THE SLEEPER

Ten years have passed since Olga Lubimova married Englishman Henry Trent and left her native Russia, so why is she still unable to take her freedom for granted? Following a dinner party given by photographer Hugo Stratton, a cold voice on the telephone plunges Olga intio a nightmare. There is no hiding place from those who threaten her children – until Hugo's lifestyle catches up with him and Olga can run headlong into the custody awaiting his murderer. It seems an open-and-shut case, but senior officers are bewildered when orders are given for a secret murder hunt...

THE SLEEPER

THE SLEEPER

by

Eileen Dewhurst

Dales Large Print Books
Long Preston, North Yorkshire,
BD23 4ND, England.

British Library Cataloguing in Publication Data.

Dewhurst, Eileen
    The sleeper.

    A catalogue record of this book is
    available from the British Library

    ISBN   978-1-84262-610-8 pbk

First published in Great Britain 1988
by William Collins Sons & Co. Ltd.

Copyright © Eileen Dewhurst 1988

The moral right of the author has been asserted

Published in Large Print 2008 by arrangement with
Eileen Dewhurst, care of Gregory & Company

Dales Large Print is an imprint of Library Magna Books Ltd.

Printed and bound in Great Britain by
T.J. (International) Ltd., Cornwall, PL28 8RW

Part One

CHAPTER 1

'But, Hugo, it isn't quite as simple as that. There's the question of the principle involved…'

Olga watched her husband in affectionate amusement as he leaned across the dinner table towards their host, blinking rapidly a number of times in the way which always announced the importance to him of the point he was about to make.

'I know, Henry, I know, and the knowledge pains me. So may we talk about my latest fancy photograph instead?'

Hugo had side-stepped a serious discussion so outrageously even Henry smiled as he gave up and leaned back in his chair. Hugo's latest girlfriend, a large handsome creature with one eye permanently obscured by her honey blonde hair, continued to look sultry. Really, reflected Olga as she netted Henry's smile and returned it, there was only the girl's preening at Hugo's absent-minded but regular compliments to indicate that she was aware of her surroundings. Hugo's girlfriends were never notable for their powers of speech or of intellect, but Samantha seemed even more passive than the norm...

Hugo was asking her if she would like a little more zabaglione.

'No, thank you, Hugo dear. But it was lovely.'

As always in company, Olga was reluctantly aware of the unEnglish precision of her voice. She had shed her accent within the first two or three years of her marriage, but it seemed she was unable to lose what sounded, in her own ears, like pedantic correctness of speech. Sometimes she spoke her exasperation aloud to Henry, and then he told her that her voice speaking English was the first part of her he had fallen in love with and that he was relieved, as her pronunciation improved, to realize that it was not going to lose its uniqueness.

'I'm glad you found it lovely, Olga darling.' Hugo was mocking her. Fondly, because he liked both her and the way she spoke. And there was a noticeable precision in his own voice, about which Henry, after they'd spent any time with Hugo, tended to remark that what had begun as an affectation had ended as a reflex.

'Samantha my pretty? Henry? No? Then let's adjourn. No, Olga, I positively forbid you to take so much as a teaspoon out to the kitchen. I refuse to spoil the evening by any reference to the unacceptable face of gastronomy, and anyway I expect Sam will help me later.'

Olga found it difficult to imagine the decorative Samantha assisting Hugo to wash dishes, but he had no doubt mentioned the likelihood of it merely in order to make them aware that Samantha would not be leaving the flat when she and Henry did.

'Schoolboy Stratton strikes again,' whispered Henry, as he stood aside to let her follow Samantha's swaying progress back into the sitting-room. He raised his voice. 'So where's this photograph, Hugo?'

'Ah yes.' Hugo crossed the room as his guests sat down, to draw forward the shrouded easel Olga had noticed in its usual corner. Hugo was joint proprietor of a fashionably successful photographic studio in Kew, but maintained an ambition to leave a unique æsthetic mark on the world in the manner of Cecil Beaton. He had once, towards the end of a rather bibulous party, confided this ambition to Olga in something like these words, but he had never mentioned it again. Suspecting that if he remembered what he had said he was regretting it as the expression of an earnestness he always affected to despise, she herself had not referred to it except to Henry. But there was nearly always, mounted on the easel in Hugo's flat, some idiosyncratic photograph or photo collage to enable his friends to put two and two together.

Hugo had paused behind the sofa, at the usual spot for his unveiling. 'It's called The Diptych.' He whipped off the black velvet cloth in a dramatic gesture, moving his eyes over his visitors as he did so to note their reactions. Olga shivered and wished Henry's hand was within holding distance. Henry blinked a few times, and Samantha squeaked 'Hugo!' in a rather high voice before asking, in a deeper tone, who the model was.

'It took quite a bit of setting up,' said Hugo modestly, ignoring the question. 'Well?'

His glance had stopped at Olga. Reluctantly she studied the big black and white rectangle in front of them. 'It's brilliant, Hugo. But I can't say I like it. It's – it's so Beardsley.'

'Thank you, Olga. I knew you'd deliver.'

The centrepiece of Hugo's photograph was a seated young woman facing straight on to the camera, as beautiful as Samantha but in an entirely different way – dark with noticeable bones. To her right was a background group of people with clothes and countenances clearly suggesting goodness. The group to the left of her was a mob, Bosch figures in all but their modern dress, leering and writhing together as if – Olga would have to have gone closer, under a more searching light, to be certain – taking part in

10

an orgy. But what had made her shiver was the woman in the foreground. The right half of her was grave and decorous, the hair neatly unremarkable, the make-up unobtrusive, the long-sleeved dark dress covering the knee above a dark-stockinged leg ending in a court shoe, the hand held by a background girl of markedly angelic expression. On the left side the hair was wild and spiky, the face paint outrageous, the breast half bare above an unbuttoned blouse and a minimal tight skirt straining where the leg stretched out towards the mob which was just grasping the ankle-strapped sandal. The expression on the subject's face, as well, was divided into two. On the right it was calm and serious, on the left the mouth stretched in a knowing smile.

'I didn't expect it to be liked,' said Hugo. Glad to look away from the photograph, Olga turned to him and decided that in his own way he presented as ambivalent an image as his creation. She and Henry knew him to be warm and kind, ingenuous even in some of his reactions, but they were aware, from observation and from Hugo's own regular intimations, of other aspects of his character. Even the look of him, despite his slender grace and sensitive features under the heavy mane of dark gold hair, could change in a moment from prince through elf to satyr... 'It's two photographs, of course. I got the crowd through a theatrical agent friend, and they played the good guys and the mob.' Hugo chuckled reminiscently. 'I had a Good Day and a Bad.' He pronounced the capital letters. 'That was because of the costumes and make-up and lighting and so on, of course, but it was interesting how it affected the atmosphere. On the Bad Day everyone was so much naughtier and more aggressive. Annabel, in all fairness, seemed happier as the good girl.'

'Annabel?' repeated Samantha.

'My model,' said Hugo, not looking at her. 'Of course, the whole of her was made up for the good girl, then for the bad. Then I took half of each picture and put them together. Effective, isn't it?'

'Very,' said Henry. 'In fact, quite a statement, Hugo. The struggle for the human soul.'

'Well, yes.' Olga thought Hugo was suddenly evasive, but he was facing another risk of being taken seriously. 'If you like. I said I was calling it The Diptych, but I'm not sure Jana wouldn't be better. Short and sweet.'

'Jana...' said Samantha lingeringly. 'I don't think I've heard that name before.' For the first time she had strung sufficient words together for Olga to note that her voice was careful mid-Atlantic.

'I don't suppose you have, sweetie.' Hugo

tossed her a quick smile. 'Seeing that it's my own invention. Janus, the two-faced man. Jana, the two-faced woman. Yes?'

'It's quite good,' said Olga. 'A nice sound, and easier to say than The Diptych.' Certainly so far as she herself was concerned.

'Jana it shall be, then,' said Hugo, giving her a little bow. 'I'd wondered whether to involve you at an earlier stage, Olga.' Olga was aware of a sudden nestling movement from the chair beside her where Samantha sat. 'Then decided to keep it all for myself. But you see, even at this stage, you've been helpful. And now, I think, coffee.'

With another showman's gesture Hugo veiled his photograph in the velvet cloth and pushed the easel towards its corner.

'It should have quite an impact,' said Henry, Olga thought reluctantly. 'Could even become a symbol for our times.'

'You think so?' Hugo hastened out of the corner, looking now like a schoolboy with his flushed eager face.

'I think it's possible. I mean … it's a very strong image.'

'Thank you, Henry!'

Humming *It's a Lovely Day Today,* Hugo pranced out to the kitchen, waving away Samantha's gesture of half rising to accompany him.

'Has Hugo used you for a model yet, Samantha?' asked Olga into the immediately obtrusive silence. 'You're so very photo-genic, I'm sure he–'

'Not yet,' said Samantha.

'He does, of course, generally employ pro-fessional models,' went on Olga, not know-ing if she was speaking the truth but wishing to be kind.

Samantha bridled again. Henry gave Olga a look which told her to leave well alone, and the loud peal on the front doorbell came as a welcome distraction.

'Could you go, dearies?' called Hugo from the kitchen.

Olga was the first one up. Henry followed her to the front door.

On the step was a young woman who just by standing there made her fall back against Henry's trembling arm. Jana, now, had reached the middle way, a fusion of the two sides of her which Hugo had presented. Her hair was untidy without being deliberately wild, her face was strained with anxiety, and she wore trousers.

'Where's Hugo?' she asked breathlessly, then, Olga thought, tried to pull herself together under their concerned gaze.

'You'd better come in,' said Olga, glancing involuntarily towards the open sitting-room door. Samantha, rather in the way a statue might come to life, was rising slowly to her feet. 'Hugo! It's – it's Jana.'

'I'm Annabel Gordon,' said the girl as she

crossed the threshold, her face unchanging. Evidently Hugo hadn't shared with her his meditations over the title of his photograph.

'Goodness me!' Hugo was bustling in a fussy way across the hall. 'What a surprise, Annie!'

'Annie?' queried Samantha, making Olga aware she was now in the hall.

'I see I'm interrupting a party, Hugo,' said Annabel Gordon, her eyes on Samantha. 'It's so long since I heard from you I thought you must be dead or away.' Her gaze turned on him, pleading.

'Sorry, dear,' said Hugo. His own eyes were sparkling and Olga, with another involuntary shiver, saw his dark side in her realization that he was enjoying what he ought to be deploring. 'I do happen to have been most frightfully busy. I'll ring you tomorrow.'

The dark-haired girl looked round the motionless group and lowered her eyes. She was suddenly ashamed, and Olga painfully sorry for her. 'I shouldn't have come.'

'That's all right.' Hugo did, at least, throw a quick glance at the impassive Samantha. Then, eyes still aglow, he asked Annabel if she would like some coffee.

Olga heard Henry's sharp breath.

'No, thank you, Hugo.' The second young woman had regained her dignity. 'I only called in because I was nearby. I'm – glad you're all right.'

'I'll be in touch.' Hugo looked slightly crestfallen, then brightened. 'We've been looking at the photograph. Henry here thinks it may be heading for posterity.'

'Does he?' The eyes, veiled Olga thought by suffering, glanced at Henry indifferently.

The doorbell rang again.

'Well, now!' said Hugo, pulling it inward with a flourish.

On the step was a dark thin young man with an angry white face. The only person in the hall to react was Annabel Gordon. She said 'Roger!' as she moved further away from the door.

'I knew where you'd be!' The young man, without invitation, stepped into the hall, and shrugging his shoulders Hugo closed the door behind him.

'You're the last, I hope,' he observed.

'I'm the last man you're going to ride roughshod over, Mr Stratton!'

'Oh dear,' said Hugo. His eyes were still bright, but Olga noticed there was at last wariness in the glance he shifted from Annabel to Samantha. 'I don't have the pleasure...'

'I know you, Mr Stratton.' Yes, not much likelihood of a mistake. Olga smiled to herself. Her scholarly, ascetic-looking Henry could never be mistaken for a Hugo Stratton. 'I'm Roger Innes.'

'I'm afraid I'm still...' Hugo's expression

of bewilderment grew more elaborate.

'Annabel's boyfriend.'

'Ah!' Hugo now smiled round at each member of the group in turn, but Olga was aware of his increasing discomfort. 'I'm very glad to meet you, Roger. Annabel has been a simply splendid model. I told her I'd find another interesting job for her, and I've taken so long, been so busy, she came to remind me of my promise.' At least, Olga learned with relief, there was a point beyond which Hugo was not prepared to go. 'As you're here, do let me show you the photograph I took of Annabel, my friends have just been—'

'Not now, thanks.' But he had calmed down. 'Are you ready, Annabel?'

'Yes.' Annabel Gordon moved towards the door, looking at Hugo. 'So if there is a job, Hugo...' she murmured. Olga, on another pang of pity, decided she was doing the best she could.

'I think there may be,' said Hugo encouragingly, offering a wide impersonal smile. Olga saw the girl wince. 'As I said, I'll ring you.'

'All right,' she whispered, and the young man said a loud good night, drawing her out of the flat and closing the door sharply behind them.

'Well,' said Hugo, going up to Samantha and putting an arm across her shoulders.

'Excitement over.'

'Time we were on our way, too,' said Henry. Samantha hadn't so much shaken Hugo's arm off as just started walking back into the sitting-room.

'That's nonsense, Henry, you haven't had coffee. Or a brandy. I have some rather special brandy.' Hugo followed Samantha, who was now sitting down again, her face without expression. 'Brandy for you, darling?'

'I'll have Cointreau if you've got it.' The slow voice was blank, too. Olga found herself uncharacteristically regretting that she would not be able to observe Samantha's behaviour after she and Henry had left the flat. It would be interesting to discover whether or not the girl was exercising self-control.

'Of course, Sam. And coffee all round?'

Without waiting for an answer Hugo went swiftly from the room. Stifling her strong desire to follow him, Olga sat down and asked Samantha what she did.

'Receptionist/secretary.' Samantha studied her long rosy nails, evoking for Olga the image of a brushful of varnish poised above them while a member of the public coughed for attention.

'That must be interesting.' As always, Olga wished her voice didn't give so much weight to insincere remarks. 'In a hotel?'

'Yeah.'

'In London, I suppose?' contributed Henry.

'That's right, yeah.'

'Here we are!'

Hugo came in carrying a laden tray, which he set down on the low centre table. 'Would you like to pour, Olga, while I get the liqueurs?'

He spoke automatically as he walked across to the cupboard where he kept his drinks. Despite the *de rigueur* presence of an attractive girl, it was always Olga he asked to pour the after-dinner coffee. Samantha made another sharp little nestling movement. Olga thought she had noticed them because for the rest of the time the girl sat so still.

She was surprised that the remainder of the evening went so comfortably, but Hugo had no doubt produced a great deal of adrenalin to cope with his uninvited guests, and had enough left to carry his official visitors along with his one-man cabaret until Olga's thoughts of her children grew insistent enough to bring her to her feet.

Ignoring Hugo's pursuing protests, she carried the coffee tray out to the kitchen, where as always she was surprised at the order he had restored without appearing to spend any time away from them.

'That was a near one,' she observed, as she

set the tray down on the clean bare centre table.

'What do you mean?' asked Hugo innocently, as she turned to look at him. She was a tall woman, and he only a little above average male height, so that they were almost face to face. Under her gaze his eyes wavered, the smiling certainty left his mouth. 'I don't like second best,' he said shortly. 'So I go for something completely different.'

'But, Hugo, it doesn't have to be third best, either.' Surprised, she searched his face. It had never occurred to her – or, she thought, to Henry – that Hugo might be nursing a lost or unrequited love.

'Doesn't it?' Now he was studying her, with an open affection which killed the stab of anxiety even as she was aware of it. So far as she was concerned, the appearance of things must be the truth of them.

'I'm sorry, Hugo, it's none of my business. I suppose it's just that Henry and I are so happy, we can't help wishing–'

'Do you both really think that I'm unhappy? Dear Olga, we all want different things.' Hugo was smiling again, the moment of truth had passed.

'Not unhappy exactly, Hugo…You're quite right, I was committing the bossy woman's sin of wanting other people to be happy *her* way.'

'That's not you, Olga.' Hugo put his hands

on her shoulders and kissed her cheek. 'That is the provincial lady, and you are a cosmopolitan. I cherish your cold approval of my new work of art.'

'Thank you for good company, Hugo, and a splendid dinner as always.' She didn't feel insincere, their host had offered more good company than was normally to be expected from host and hostess combined.

'I love you and Henry to come. Come again soon.' Henry now was standing beside them. Beyond him, across the hall, Olga saw Samantha framed in the sitting-room doorway.

'That is an even more beautiful picture than yours,' said Olga, laughing and pointing, glad of the opportunity to offer some genuine compliment to Hugo's other artefact.

'Sam. Ah yes.' Hugo brought their coats out of the cloakroom, helped Olga into hers, then crossed the hall to put his arm round Samantha and draw her forward. With a mixture of relief and exasperation Olga saw that she now leaned noticeably against him.

'Goodbye,' said Samantha. 'Nice meeting you.'

'And you,' said Olga and Henry together.

'Oh, that funny naughty book!' said Hugo, his hand out to the door. 'I'll just get it for you, Henry. If it doesn't make you laugh out loud I shall bake myself a marzipan hat and eat it. Hang on a moment.'

'Thank you, Hugo.'

An item from Hugo's cabaret had consisted of memorized excerpts from a humorous book he had recently discovered. In his mouth they had been funny, but Olga suspected he was keener to lend than Henry to borrow. As Hugo darted away Samantha swayed like a flower in the breeze of his quick departure, then stood rooted to the spot where he had left her.

'Here we are!' Hugo handed the book to Henry as Samantha slowly seized his other arm. 'Keep it as long as you like, I know it by heart.'

'Hugo seems about to get more than he deserves,' observed Henry in the car.

'It looks like it.' Thinking of Samantha, Olga made her own nestling movement into the comfortable seat, glad to be alone and on the way home with Henry. 'I wish he'd find someone … well…'

'More like you?' suggested Henry. 'I'd be glad to see it, but perhaps Hugo wouldn't.'

'That's what he said to me himself. Well, not precisely that, he said we all want different things. I suddenly wondered if he had loved and lost.'

'Did you?'

She turned to him as he made the rare gesture of taking his eyes off the road to look at her, aware of something more in his voice than his words warranted.

'Yes. Do you think it's likely?'

'I don't know, my darling. But I suspect there are many things about Hugo that I don't know.'

'For a dreadful second, Henry, I thought it might be me. Then the next minute I knew for certain that it wasn't.'

His voice came soft and serene. 'No, Olga, it isn't you.'

Pam had the front door open before they were out of the car.

'I've had a super evening,' she said on the step. 'The children were angelic and then there was lots of lovely TV. And I knew that if the telephone rang I wouldn't have to miss more than a minute, because of only having to say Mrs Trent was out and could I take a message. It didn't ring, darlings. And neither of the children made a sound once I'd said it was lights out. Did you have a good time?'

'Yes,' said Olga, wondering if they had. She put her arms round her best friend and gave her a hug. 'You are a dear. Will you have tea or something before Henry walks you home?'

'Better not.' But Pam's round cheerful face had registered temptation. 'Brian was inclined to want to come with me tonight and I didn't encourage him, I rather felt I'd enjoy the sort of time I've just had. If I'm too late it might add up to a grievance, so don't take your coat off, Henry. I'm not working tomorrow morning, Olga. See you some time?'

'I have a pupil at half-past eleven. If you would like to slip in for a coffee... Half-past ten?'

'Lovely.'

'Thank you again, Pam. Really, we had quite an amusing time.'

Before Henry and Pam had reached the gate she was upstairs looking at her sleeping son. Then moving next door to her daughter before kicking off her shoes and padding barefoot about the house, touching things as she went by. As always during the past ten years of her life, taking nothing for granted.

CHAPTER 2

'Hurry up, Martin, Daddy's waiting!'

Olga called up the stairs, as she did most weekday mornings, while Henry stood in the open front doorway as close to impatience as he could get, hand in hand with the well-organized Lucy.

'I don't know why he takes so long,' said Lucy, a little too smugly for Olga's taste.

'You get help,' she said, turning away from the stairs to settle the blue velour hat more securely on her daughter's head. 'Martin's so old now he has to do things for himself.' Her hand stayed on Lucy's face, smoothing the strands of fair hair across her forehead and down over her ears.

'He's eight. I'm only six.'

'Miss Clever Clogs. Will we see you at the usual time this evening?' she asked Henry. To each side of his tall thin figure, which was beginning to shift from foot to foot as the minutes ticked away, the corners of the front garden were still mysterious and soft-edged in the remains of the mist which when Olga had drawn back the curtains had been white drifts of fog across the mono-chrome suburban lawns.

'I hope so. We've an extraordinary meeting this afternoon but it begins at two and I can't imagine– Ah, here you are at last, Martin.'

'Sorry, Dad. Goodbye, Mum.' Martin had not used the extra time to improve the appearance he had presented at the breakfast table, and Olga caught him by the tie as he attempted to whirl past her.

'That's better.' She had straightened it, and pulled his jacket properly on to his shoulders before smoothing his thick straight hair. 'Mrs Porteous is doing the school run today, I'll see you both back here.'

'What's for tea?' called Lucy over her shoulder.

'I haven't made up my mind. Be happy and good!'

'Come on, Dad,' shouted Martin from the car. Henry was kissing Olga. 'I'm monitor this week. I mustn't be late.'

'Don't blame me,' said Henry mildly as he scrunched across the gravel. 'Although I'll blame you if I miss my train.'

Olga watched the car out of sight, a ritual she had adopted since Lucy, at the start of the autumn term just a week ago, had begun to stay at school all day. Turning slowly back into the house, she was glad to think of the morning being broken by a French lesson, it would shorten the time until half-past four and Lucy at last home again... She must snap out of it; she had promised herself to do some extra reading and more work on her translations in the afternoons when they became her own, and as the cosmopolitan rather than the provincial woman Hugo had called her last night she should be relishing the prospect, not feeling forlorn because her daughter was growing up.

Olga quickened her pace into the kitchen and set about tidying and superficially cleaning it. Mrs Metcalfe would be in the next morning to 'bottom out', as she expressed it, so the process didn't take long and Olga was soon on her way upstairs. Sometimes she felt self-indulgent for using Mrs Metcalfe to make her comfortable life even more comfortable, but it had been Henry's idea initially to employ her, and Henry who insisted, in the face of Olga's periodic suggestions that she could manage on her own, that she should be kept on. And Mrs Metcalfe was, of course, a reliable child-sitter – more often than Pam could be expected to oblige...

Lucy's room was almost tidy, but as usual Olga spent more time there than among Martin's long-suffering belongings, enjoying thoughts of her daughter moving contentedly about her private kingdom as she contrasted Lucy's life with her memories of her own nervous childhood in the crowded Moscow flat.

But this morning images of Hugo, his uncomfortable photograph, and the two girls and the boy he had disturbed, dominated her more usual musings as she moved about the house, pausing regularly, as she always did, at windows. From Martin's window at the front she could just see Pam's house across the deep curve of The Crescent – like the far end of a stationary train, she sometimes imagined, on a looping rural route. At least, she could see part of the grey-green roof and a chimney stack, rising above the trees and bushes still in full leaf which surrounded the Franklin front garden. By her own bedroom window at the back, where she came to a longer stop, Olga stood looking abstractedly down the garden she and Henry had made, wishing she had been able to persuade Hugo the night before to say more about the side of himself she could never understand. About why he chose Samanthas, for instance. Pam, to whom he was a bit of a joke (but then Hugo hadn't much time for Pam, either), tended to make fun of the air of mystery with which Hugo surrounded himself. Not that they really knew one another, they had scarcely met apart from the dinner party to which she and Henry had invited them both in the selfish and unrealized hope that, having friendship with their hosts in common, they might discover other points of agreement too. Pam had said...

Pam. She was coming in for coffee in half an hour, and there was still some work to be done for the first tutorial at eleven-thirty.

Olga turned swiftly from the window and ran out of the room. She was on the stairs when the telephone rang, and stopped half way while she decided to answer it upstairs rather than down. The absurdity of the dilemma amused her and, back in her bedroom, she was smiling as she lifted the receiver.

'Olga Trent?'

'Yes?' She didn't recognize the man's voice, cold, quiet and clear.

'Wife of Henry Trent?'

'Yes.' Afterwards, she remembered that her fear had begun with the man's second question. 'Who is that?'

'You are alone?'

'Yes... Who *is* that?'

'It does not matter who I am, Olga Lubimova.' Through the window, now, the garden was drawing pastel colour from the struggling emergence of the late September sun, a pale yellow circle breaking the overall white dazzle of the sky. Entering her eyes as the terror entered her ears, it was a picture which would never be forgotten.

'I don't...'

'You will listen, please. Carefully. You are listening, Olga Lubimova?' There was a pause, in which the garden seemed to move

29

away from the house. 'Olga Lubimova?'

'Yes – yes, I'm listening.' When she had first tried to answer no voice had come. And then, as if the ten years had never been, she had thought to answer in Russian.

'We have been generous, you have been given plenty of time in which to become a respectable British citizen. It is time now for you to begin your work for your own country.'

'I don't...' The sun had come fully clear of the cloud and was slanting across Henry's cherished lawn, throwing a sharp black point of shadow beyond the cupressus they had planted to soften the impact of next door's shed wall. How could this thing be happening in a world of cupressus and garden sheds?

'Perhaps we have left you too long, Olga Lubimova. Please pull yourself together. And listen. This telephone call is to remind you of your undertaking, and to tell you that you will soon hear from us again with specific details of your first assignment. I need hardly remind you, I think, that you have two young children. Olga Lubimova?'

'You need hardly remind me, no,' said Olga, hearing with a sort of astonishment her own suddenly cold, clear voice.

'Good. You will continue in your normal way. You will not speak to your husband. Or to anyone else.'

'I will not.'

'Good.' Only the man's words conveyed approbation or disapproval. There was nothing in the tone. 'That is all.'

She heard the click, then the continuous harsh purr of the disconnection. When she had eventually replaced her receiver she climbed on to the smooth surface of the bed she had made in the world so abruptly ended, and curled up on her side like a foetus, her hands two fists under her chin.

So it had come. The call to service she had been told to expect when, radiant with joyous astonishment, she had also been told she was to receive a visa permitting her to leave the Soviet Union for the United Kingdom, to live there with the British engineer for whom she had acted as interpreter and then married at the Moscow Palace of Weddings. Neither she nor Henry had dared hope for the visa so early in their marriage, and the secret condition on which it was granted had scarcely penetrated the dazzle of relief and delight which had surrounded her.

It had been different for a while after she had come to England, after the first enchanted passionate weeks in Henry's tiny flat in central London, when he had found the house in The Crescent at Kew and they had taken his mother's fine furniture out of store and moved in. After that there had been time to think, to realize that the condition was as much a fact as the visa and what it had done for her...

The telephone call had so stricken her her body was hurting as well, and it was painful to roll on to her other side to lie looking out on the tree-tops and the pale sun and sky. After they had moved into the house there had been nights on that bed when she had been unable to sleep and had lain rigidly motionless, willing Henry not to wake and force her to act as if there were no longer any cares in her world. She would have to act now.

It was hard to say when she had started to relax, to cease to dread the telephone, the unfamiliar envelope through the letterbox, seeing the same person twice on the underground, a man on a park bench behind a newspaper. Gradually, though, she had drawn a sort of illogical hope from the very fact of time passing, and then there had been a baby to expect. And then another.

I need hardly remind you that you have two young children.

She was trying so fiercely to contract the circle of her body she had cramped her thigh and must let go. When she sat up she saw the woman next door, wearing a flower-splashed dressing-gown, go into her greenhouse. The greenhouse was dominated by an enormous vine, from which her neighbour had once brought her a bunch of purple grapes with a yellow bloom...

Had her fear really disappeared with the years, or had she merely buried it? When she and Henry had come to The Crescent, Janice as well as Pam had befriended her. Janice had developed cancer, and Olga had found herself adopting the metaphor of her disease: five clear years, and you can be fairly confident. Janice hadn't been granted them, but she had had ten.

Disturbed eventually by no more than the recurrent nightmare of being trapped inside a glass bubble, cut off from everyone and everything which made up her life. How unrealistic, her relief each time when she woke up!

This telephone call is to remind you of your undertaking.

She knew the KGB, she should never have forgotten it.

But if she had remembered, how could she have lived her daily life as the citizen of the United Kingdom she had legally become?

Naturalization had brought a relief which Olga saw now to have been absurd. The KGB made use of anyone, of any nationality, if they could gain a hold on them.

I need hardly remind you that you have two young children.

Whatever was required of her she would have to do. As she had had to accept the condition in the first place, even sign her name to it, when they had threatened Henry. She would have to help weaken the defences, destroy the morale, of the country she loved with such passionate gratitude, her own country...

That would be it, wouldn't it, the gaining of sensitive information through her rare ability as a native Russian speaker? Through another job as an interpreter? She would have to pretend to Henry that she wanted whatever job they found for her, her life would become a lie... Yes, that would be it, what else could there be? There was no reason for this extra, indefinable sense of apprehension far down in her mind, even more distant and more dreadful than the memories which had just been wrenched to the surface...

The doorbell shrilled, immediate illustration of what lay ahead. Suddenly Olga's overwhelming reaction was fatigue, but she slithered off the bed, scrabbled for her shoes, and walked uncertainly across the room. The bell rang again as she steadied herself by the cheval glass, and she turned for a few seconds to stare at the wide-eyed woman's face, the prominent slavic bones standing out with ugly obtrusion in the unrelieved pallor, the thick brown hair standing up untidily at the crown. Automatically smoothing it with her hands, Olga stumbled out to the landing, then down the stairs. On the front step, her face brightening from a look of defeat, was the faded little woman who collected each year for the Friends of the local children's hospital.

'Ah, Mrs Trent! I was just about to give you up.'

'I'm sorry, I was on the telephone. Just hang on a minute, will you?'

Without instruction from her mind, her body went out to the kitchen for her handbag.

'Here we are. What do I usually give you?' Once again she would be suspecting strangers, she was suspicious even of this weary, worthy little woman. 'I'm sorry, that's not really a fair question.'

'It's all right, Mrs Trent. Last year... Well... Last year you generously donated a pound.'

Olga, surprised to find her hand steady, pushed two pound coins into the tin in the woman's hand. 'Inflation!' she said, surprised as well to find she could smile.

'Oh, thank you, Mrs Trent, thank you! If everyone—'

It was the woman who jumped nervously at the sound from the gate.

'Hi there!' sang out Pam as she jaunted up the path.

'Good morning, Pam.' Olga blessed her first caller for the rehearsal. 'I'm just making my contribution to the children's hospital. Have you made yours?'

'Not yet. The collection must have begun your end of The Crescent.'

'That's right, Mrs Franklin.' The collector had glanced at the list pinned to the cardboard box she wore round her neck, full of small paper circles. 'May I suggest, as you're here...?'

Their receipts stuck to their chests, Olga and Pam went into the house, Olga regretting there had not been time to telephone Pam and plead a headache. And then there was her student... Again weariness was her overwhelming sensation, and she sat down at the kitchen table.

'What's the matter, dear heart?' Pam sat down too, leaning forward across the table, her cheerful face concerned. 'You look a bit washed out.'

If that was Pam's reading of the outward signs of her devastation, she was doing quite well. 'Just one of my headaches.' Fortunately she was known to have them.

'You should have rung me. I should be ironing anyway.'

'I wanted to see you.'

Would she ever want to see anyone again? Apart from Martin and Lucy and Henry, safe around her.

'I'll put the kettle on. You just sit there. Won't you have some aspirin?'

It was a good idea. 'In my bag in the hall.'

Pam put the kettle on, then went to get the bag. 'Here, you find them.' She put the bag on the table in front of Olga. 'You've a lesson this morning, haven't you? Shall I ring up for you and cancel?'

'No. Oh no.' She must do every least thing she could to keep the children safe, and that included acting at all times – except, it must be, sometimes when she was alone – as if nothing had changed. At all times. This wasn't the sort of secret to be shared with a best friend, although she was struggling with a longing to confide in Pam, whose small plump hand was warmly over hers. At all times... All she wanted to do, really, was to lie down and sleep, so that she wouldn't have to think of the weeks, months, and years of vigilant deceit which lay ahead. 'Thanks, Pam, but it isn't as bad as that. I'd hate to let Jonathan down, or William – he comes at five. I'll have a rest between the two of them.'

'And I'll make the coffee.' Pam withdrew her hand and bounced again to her feet. 'How were the children this morning? We had fun last night, but I promise I got their lights out almost at the ordained time.'

'The children are very well.'

And very vulnerable. Her predominant mental picture of them, now, was the one where they stood hand in hand at a quarter to four just inside the school gates, waiting to be collected. *Martin and Lucy? It's all right, Mummy's been held up and she asked me to call for you...*

'...so I wasn't sorry when Brian reminded me we had an invitation for that night from one of his colleagues which involves me going up to London in the late afternoon.'

Pam must have been speaking for several minutes. Vigilance was still to be learned. 'I'm sorry, Pam, I was listening to the hammer strokes. No, honestly, it really isn't as bad as that, and it's improving.' Olga took two tablets from the small bottle in her handbag, swallowing them down with the coffee Pam had put in front of her. 'What were you saying?'

'Not worth repeating. Just that I had an invitation to tea from that odd little lady in Ardley Grove, and was glad of an excuse.'

'The one we met at Marcia's?' It was an effort, but it was a relief to find she could still use the surface of her mind, at least, in the old way.

'That's the one. Rather demure, with very careful curls. I suppose it's only postponing the inevitable, because it was the feeling I had that she wanted to cotton on to us which made me wary, and she's bound to ask me again. D'you remember her saying she felt we ought to be friends because we were roughly the same age and lived in the same area?'

'Yes. My heart sank as well.'

'I wonder she didn't invite you too. She didn't?'

'Not yet.' Another wave of fatigue, and, it must be, something in her face for a moment, because Pam was telling her, again, that she didn't look too good.

'Are you *sure* you don't want to put your pupil off?'

'Quite sure. I expect I look tired because I didn't sleep as well as usual. There were one or two things at Hugo's last night...' She could talk about Hugo's dinner party to her one confidante. And less than an hour ago it had been her chief preoccupation.

'I suppose the party was made up by one of his brainless beauties?' Pam looked as scathing as her friendly face allowed.

'Oh, yes. Samantha, this one. But there was another one. Uninvited.'

'Tell me!' Pam made a snuggling movement into her chair, reminding Olga of Hugo's official girlfriend of the night before. Was it only the night before that she had met Samantha?

'It was a bit strange, really.' She was having to make a savage effort of memory, as if dredging up a recollection from long ago. 'Hugo showed us his latest photo collage, which was disturbing enough in itself, and then the doorbell rang and I answered it as Hugo was in the kitchen. It was the girl from the collage, obviously upset because she hadn't seen Hugo for too long. And Samantha unnerved me in a different way because she didn't show any reactions of any kind. Then the second girl's boyfriend arrived in furious pursuit of her.' Olga paused, not wanting to fuel Pam's dislike of Hugo by telling her that he had enjoyed the confrontations. 'That was all, really, but it was somehow on my mind and I was thinking about it instead of going to sleep.'

Olga was able to glance at the clock on the wall without turning her head, but Pam saw the movement of her eyes and got to her feet, picking up both coffee mugs and going across to the sink to rinse them.

'I must be off. You've only got twenty minutes before whoever it is arrives to guzzle your pearls of wisdom.'

'It's all right, but there are one or two things I should look up.' Whatever Pam did, reflected Olga, watching the stocky body move briskly in front of the draining-board as the quick hands dried it down, she gave an impression of cheerful energy. While Pam was playing hockey and lacrosse at her boarding-school Olga had been walking the long Moscow distances – for some reason her mind swerved away from what was usually the least forbidding of her Russian memories – but ten years in Britain had made her privy to a number of British myths, and it was easy to picture schoolgirl Pam illustrating the amusing phrase 'jolly hockey-sticks'. There was much more to Pam, though, than that. Warmth and kindness and humour. If only she could talk to her…

She got to her feet as Pam turned round.

'Well, I'm off.' Pam came back to the table and put her arms lightly round Olga so that the top of her soft hair tickled Olga's chin. It was an effort to restrain her own responding embrace.

'Thanks for coming, and making the coffee. I'm fine now. See you soon.'

As she walked to the front door, Olga realized that despite the strain of behaving as if this monstrous thing hadn't happened, she didn't want Pam to go. When she was alone she would have no vital reason for holding the horror at bay.

CHAPTER 3

'*J'ai peur que vous ne preniez froid,*' said Olga slowly into the polite face on the other side of the dining table. 'I am afraid you may catch cold.' *I am afraid we may catch our deaths.* 'I am afraid, Jonathan, that the use of the subjunctive in French is difficult for the English to grasp. But there is at least a logic to it, as there is to most aspects of the French language. Possibility. Doubt. You may catch cold, you may not.' *They may or may not carry out their threat.*

'I think I understand that, Mrs Trent, but the half negative's puzzling.'

'I know. Try and think of it as expressing the may/may not, the ambiguity.' *I don't have to remind you that you have two young children…* She wasn't going to be able to live in the two worlds at the same time, so she must discipline her thoughts to stay in the old one when she was with other people, that was the first, the most essential, thing she must learn to do. 'And, of course, a French idiomatic usage. Which means that it needs learning by heart. That's the only thing to do, really, when one can't parallel in English.'

'Yes, I know.' The young man gave a gusty sigh, then resumed smiling. 'But it *is* beginning to make sense at last, Mrs Trent, I'm awfully grateful.'

'It gives me pleasure too you know, Jonathan, to see you improve.' Last week, it had done. 'You'll get that GCSE next summer.' Next summer... What would she be doing next summer? Merely to survive until then, self-discipline was vital. For the family to survive...

Olga got up so hurriedly the chair rocked behind her. 'We'll leave it there for today, Jonathan. Try to look during the week at the notes you've taken. Several times for a few minutes is best for absorbing things. You can choose our passages for translation next week. Is your mother better?'

'Better than she was, thanks, Mrs Trent.' Jonathan was on his feet, too, gathering his books together, dropping one in his eagerness to be out of her way now she had declared the lesson over. As always, so polite.

Trained to be polite, to present the image of an ingenuous young man who wanted no more from her than a good French GCSE?

That way paranoia lay. She had even jumped, made a little moaning sound, as the boy jerked out his hand to save another book from falling.

'What is it, Mrs Trent?'

'Just a crick in my neck, I must have slept

awkwardly. It will ease as the day goes on.'

If only the day didn't have to go on. If only she could go upstairs now and lie down, and not wake up again. Surely, then, they would leave the children alone?

'I can tell there's something.' Jonathan was anxiously studying her face, and she forced her mouth into a smile.

'I'm all right, Jonathan. Really. A stiff neck can give quite a sharp pain, and that can make one tired. I'll see you next week.'

When she had shut the front door on him she sat down on the chair beside it, weak with the new shock of finding herself contemplating suicide.

And why not, she continued. With pills it would be easy and painless, and she could do it in such a way that everyone – that Henry – would think it had been an accident. Henry would suffer, but he would recover. As would the children...

In the kitchen, without being aware of having walked there, Olga looked round in surprise at the evidences of an ordinary life. At the mustard and cress flourishing on the ledge above the sink, the latest artistic efforts of the children pinned to the back of the door, the row of brightly coloured cereal packets next to the toaster, the cat's saucer almost empty of milk...

The cat. All at once she longed for the comfort of the cat, the feel of his fur re-

sponding to her hand, the sound of his purring. She hadn't seem him since breakfast. If
anything had happened to him…Would they
– could they, even they? – start that way?
Give her a sample, as it were, of how it would
be if she failed to do as she was told?

Olga ran across the kitchen and wrenched
open the back door.

Again she couldn't use her voice, couldn't
call him, but there was no need, he was
there, sitting perversely on a spot by the
dustbins so unattractive it was almost as if
he had selected it as a penance, contemplating the boundary bushes and not even
twitching an ear as she rushed towards him.

'Tommy! Oh, Tommy!'

Olga lifted the cat into her arms and
carried him indoors, where she pulled a
chair out from the kitchen table with her
foot and sat down with him on her lap,
rubbing her chin in the soft fur of his neck
until his black body started vibrating.

'When you're dead,' she told him, 'you
can't see or hear.' In a sort of anger she stared
out on the garden, her eyes recording every
detail as a dazzling significance of shape and
colour. To a condemned man, would his cell
that last morning turn into Aladdin's cave?
The cat's purring was so sensuously lovely it
was swelling like music in her ears. The
prospect of death was an hallucinogen.

'If I'm dead, Tommy,' she went on, 'I can't

be made to–' It occurred to her that a device could have been planted in the kitchen to net any confidences she might be tempted to make – a device which would reveal her confidante to be male, but not dumb and furry... If there was a device in her bedroom it would record the sounds and movements she and Henry made. And what they said in their sleep.

Even in her sleep she must say nothing. Henry could hear it too, and the KGB would not differentiate between information she chose to give away and information spilled out in unconsciousness.

She would go upstairs and search the bedroom, it would be something to do. And then she would finish the translation she was half way through for Henry, and then work on her own long-term project of a new translation of the short stories of Chekov. Long-term, she had still called it that... Oh, and sometime she would have something to eat, there was a sensation in her stomach which could be hunger as well as panic.

Olga squirmed out from under the cat, who settled back on the seat without unfolding himself, and went across the kitchen and the hall and up the stairs. Her legs were heavy and she dragged herself along, but attached to each, of course, was the ball and chain of a child. If she rounded up the aspirins and related products in the house and took them with water, then the children would no longer be fetters and could be safely detached, there would be no point, even for the KGB (and they were the most practical of people) in leaving Martin and Lucy tied to a dead body. Whereas if she went on stumbling about with them fastened to her, and put a foot wrong...

She had known as she stroked the cat that she would not be able to kill herself, and pausing in her bedroom doorway she took a deep breath.

Relief? she asked, appalled, and had to answer yes.

But there was, of course, no alternative escape. By rejecting suicide she was accepting the role the KGB had devised for her, there wasn't a third way.

Olga ran her hands over the undersurfaces of all the furniture in her bedroom. It was easier not to think, she found, while physically occupied. In the night she would want Henry to make love to her, and as she warmed her chilled spirit in the small ray of anticipation, she saw that she could interpose it between herself and the progress of the nightmare. *Nothing more can happen until after Henry...* And then, until after she had seen everyone out of the house. One thing at least she could be sure of: she would be contacted only when she was alone at home. (And they would know.) So it was only in her solitary daytime that she need dread the telephone, when Henry and the children were with her she could relax...

Relax! Sitting back on her heels beside the bed, Olga laughed aloud. When Henry and the children were with her she would be on stage.

It was pointless to try and remember the last time someone with accredited entry had been in the house – telephone engineer, plumber, meter reader. The people who were preparing her for use would not need to ring her doorbell, if they had decided to plant devices they would have planted them. Her search had revealed nothing, and the telephone looked and felt as it always did, but she must still behave as if her every word and movement were being recorded.

Olga went slowly downstairs to the kitchen, painstakingly made herself a salad. Eating it at the kitchen table beside the sleeping cat, she found she was still looking for a way out. What if she wrote it all down, put her finger to Henry's lips and then to her own, led him by the hand to the lavatory, gave him the sheets of paper, shut him in to read them?

And then he would come tearing out in shock, from the impact of what he saw as her madness if not her dilemma, and then when she led him out to the car so that they could drive away and talk about it without fear of being overheard, whoever was watching would see the expression of their faces. And follow the car.

And perhaps have a little word with Lucy. *Did your Mummy and Daddy seem different from usual this morning?*

She was unable to kill herself so there was nothing she could do. If she made herself grasp that, she might at least conserve some energy to withstand the rest of her life. To behave as if it hadn't changed out of recognition. To deceive Henry. That, of course, was the supreme test. If she could do that, she could do everything else.

She no longer wanted to lie down, she wanted to get out of the house. When she had locked the back door she shrugged into a jacket and went out of the front and round the bend in the drive to the gate, forcing herself to glance about her no more than she would normally do to observe the state of the front garden, her ears unnaturally alert to distinguish between the sounds of blackbird scolds and skirmishes in the bushes, and the sounds of hidden men.

Someone was bound to be following her. Well, she would be seen to be alone, and the choice of a solitary walk after what she had learned would surely be taken as a sign of sense rather than of weakness.

Appropriately, the promise of the morning had foundered on an access of low cloud which now covered the sky. There was no wind to challenge it, and Olga felt no change in temperature between indoors and out. Inside a glass bubble, of course, there was no climate.

But Kew Gardens were still at hand, and even today could not entirely fail her.

'Hello, me dear, and how are *you* this morning?'

The man on the gate was the small fat one with the black moustache and pebble glasses.

'I'm very well, thank you. How are you?'

'Can't grumble, I suppose. Enjoy yourself, me dear.'

'Thank you. I always do in the Gardens.'

If there were only acquaintances to face, it would be easy.

Away from the house her body felt lighter and she was able to walk at her usual pace to the lakeside, where she lingered a while to watch the water birds swimming and preening before returning to the Broad Walk and finding a seat.

So she had sat, thought Olga, welcoming the bruise of the memory because it was to feel something other than numbness or dread, at lunch-time in Gorky Park, the day after the night Henry had told her he loved her. Then she had felt isolated from the people around her because of the uniqueness of her happiness, she had been sorry for them all because Henry did not care for them, was not going to move heaven and earth to take them to England. She, Olga Lubimova, an obscure Moscow interpreter, had been singled out for joy.

Now, in another park, she was isolated again, even though a young woman was beside her on the seat, a baby she had taken out of its pram cuddled on her lap... They had, of course, waited until Martin and Lucy were beyond the baby stage, until she had the freedom of action to carry out their orders. But not until the children were old enough for the instincts of mother love and protectiveness to have lost their primitive strength.

The baby was gurgling contentedly, stretching and waving its hands and feet. 'Is it a boy or a girl?' asked Olga.

'It's a little girl, isn't it, my precious!' The woman gave the answer to the baby rather than her neighbour, then looked up and smiled dreamily at Olga. 'I thought I wanted a boy ever so badly, but I wouldn't change Sally for the world.' For a few seconds she crooned over the baby, then awkwardly, as if prompted by a sense of social obligation to the woman who had been interested enough to speak to her, asked Olga if she had any children.

'I have one boy, one girl.'

'Lucky you!'

'Yes, I have been lucky.' And this girl,

51

perhaps, had been instructed to tempt her into speech, to report on her morale. Olga got to her feet. 'I'm afraid I must go. Goodbye.'

By setting her on the road to luck, they had begun her training...

The cat was precisely as she had left him, helping her to feel that other things were likely to be, too. She managed to hold the nightmare at bay while she made herself a pot of tea, then filled her mind with Henry's translation, which she was just finishing when she heard the children at the front door.

'Here we are!' Small dark Sadie Porteous was on the step, a hand on the shoulder of each child. Sadie Porteous who had once said – Olga remembered on a surge of gratitude and relief – that she was sharp with any of the children if she found them outside the school gates when she went to collect them. 'Safely delivered!'

As a reward for having managed to maintain the semblance of an ordinary day?

'Oh, thank you, Sadie.'

'May they come to tea with my two tomorrow? I'm doing the run again, and it's so easy ... Olga?'

'Yes, of course,' said Olga hurriedly, struggling from under the minor blow of realizing there would be days on which her worst fears would not be relieved by mid-afternoon. 'I was just thinking you're too generous, they always seem to be going to you.'

'No more often than mine come to you!' On the forecourt behind Sadie, two velour hats bobbed animatedly above the back seat of the car. 'Which reminds me, they were fighting just now, I'd better get them home. That's all right then?'

'Thank you, yes. I can come for them, I don't have a pupil on a Friday.'

'Nonsense, Olga, I'll drop them off when I go to the station for Robert.'

'Well, if you're sure...'

'Of course, it's settled. I think you're wanted in the kitchen!' Martin and Lucy each had a hand and were trying to pull her into the area of the house capable of producing something to fill the aching voids which were their insides when they got home from school.

'I'm absolutely starving!' proclaimed Martin, as Olga withdrew her hand from his in order to shut the front door.

'Me too!' Lucy led the way to the kitchen and put her satchel tidily against the leg of the table before picking up the sleeping cat. It turned round once on her knee before lapsing back into unconsciousness.

Unconsciousness?

Perhaps after all when she was out...

'What are we having, Mum?' clamoured Martin.

Dragging her eyes and her thoughts from the inert cat, Olga prepared a favourite tea, to the usual accompaniment of information and complaint about the day at school. As usual, too, Lucy sat almost still beside the table, even when (to Olga's relief) the cat got down from her knee to demand a snack, and Martin banged restlessly about the kitchen, knocking over Olga's watering-can and stepping in the cat's milk. The familiar scene was so poignant that for the first time since the telephone call Olga found her eyes were wet.

'Here you are, pets.' She set the two steaming plates on the table as Martin rasped back a chair. 'When you've finished, and washed your dishes carefully – both of you, Martin – you can go into the sitting-room and watch the television until my lesson is over.' She had to blow her nose.

'Have you got a cold, Mummy?' asked Lucy.

'Perhaps. I've certainly got one of my headaches.' It was surely sense again, rather than weakness, to provide herself with a prop this first time of meeting Henry.

'Poor Mummy. And you have a *pupil*.' Lucy picked up her knife and fork. Martin was already half way through his beans and sausages.

'It will be all right, darling.'

She was at her dressing-table, trying to

disguise some of the ravages of the day, when she heard Henry arrive.

'Olga?' As always, he called her name the instant he had shut the front door.

'Hello, Henry.' It was the first time in her life she had gone reluctantly to meet him. The first time she had not welcomed the long grave look which accompanied their reunion. At least she managed to keep her eyes on his until he leaned forward to kiss her, and to hold back the announcement of her headache until she discovered how much her appearance had changed.

He had her shoulders between his hands and was examining her face so keenly her eyes wanted to close against his gaze as if it had been too bright a light.

'Are you all right?'

'Oh dear.' She had actually managed a laugh. 'You can see, can you? Yes, I've got one of my headaches.'

'Is that what it is?' She thought there was relief in his face as he took his coat off and leaned into the cloakroom to hang it up.

'Why? Do I look *so* bad?' If he would tell her how she looked, she could try to improve on it.

'No,' he said, taking her arm and walking her towards the sitting-room. This was always a good moment of the evening, Henry pouring drinks while they exchanged news of the salient points of their days, then sitting down together with their glasses before Henry went up to see Lucy, bathed and in bed, and Olga went out to the kitchen via the study to make sure Martin hadn't got the TV on very low instead of doing his bit of homework. Such a good moment, Olga had a pang of regret that it could never come again.

'So,' she persisted as they crossed the room, 'you didn't recognize my headache?'

'I thought – think – you look weary. Hard to define. Have you had the headache all day? I thought you usually woke up with them, and you seemed all right when I left.'

'I don't always wake up with them these days. It came on mid-morning, but I managed the lessons. I'm due for another couple of aspirins, but I'll have a whisky, it won't hurt.'

'Yes, have a whisky. You didn't appear to have too much to drink last night at Hugo's, but I suppose it could have brought on the headache?' With one of his heart-stopping smiles Henry turned away to the drinks cupboard, and Olga collapsed on to the sofa. So far so good. One thing she hadn't reckoned with, though, was the strength of her resistance to deceiving Henry, which was running through her like a nausea. To deceive someone who trusted you was a form of betrayal. She had promised for better or for worse.

This, of course, was the horror of political

blackmail. Relying on the one loyalty which was unshakable, it forced its victims to set aside all others...

With an agonizing effort, Olga pushed the new world away.

'I suppose it could,' she said, managing to sound reflective. 'I never really know how much wine I drink when we have dinner with Hugo, there are so many distractions. Thank you, darling.'

She took the glass from Henry's hand. Although he was still faintly smiling she was aware of the continued keenness of his blue-eyed gaze, and that it held an unwelcome hint of question. Well, she must take it as a challenge.

'Anything special today?' she asked him. 'Was the extraordinary meeting extraordinary?'

'No.' She had been waiting for his usual next move – to sit down beside her and hold her hand – so that she could be released from scrutiny, but tonight he took the chair at right angles to the sofa so that they must continue to look at one another.

'Pam came in for coffee this morning,' she said through the shaft of alarm. 'Oh yes, you knew that, didn't you? Then there was Jonathan, of course, and after lunch I went for a walk in the Gardens. The weather was disappointing but I'm always so happy there...' It would be as bad, and as uncharacteristic, to talk too much as not to talk at all. But she was afraid, now, of silence. With *Henry*.

Olga passed her hand across her forehead. 'I suppose you felt the air might clear your head,' suggested Henry. 'I thought you preferred to lie down.'

'I do when it's really bad.' He shouldn't be making it so hard for her, she thought unreasonably, even in his ignorance his instincts should spare her. 'Today I just felt like walking. Are you going up to Lucy?'

'Yes.'

She had brought this precious time together to a too early close, and as he got up Henry was giving her another keen look.

'I'll get on with the dinner.' Olga tried to make her smile spread to her eyes.

'You're sure you're up to it?' As she got to her feet he put his hand on her shoulder, and it took another savage effort not to fling herself against him.

'Don't worry, I'm up to it. It's cottage pie and it's only to be brought out of the oven.'

The meal was difficult, but fortunately during the day Henry had had the sort of discussion Hugo had denied him the night before, and wanted to talk about it. Afterwards there was an interesting documentary on television followed by a rather good play. At first Olga was wary when Henry uncharacteristically suggested they should sit together on the sofa rather than their usual chairs, but found some consolation in being able to caress his hand in wordless apology for having to deceive him.

Television, she decided, would be the best aid available for helping her to forget herself and her future, although once she thought she heard a sound overhead and had run out of the room and upstairs before she could remind herself to go gently. Both children were asleep.

In bed, of course, Henry – who had never been a victim of the diplomatic headache – respected her indisposition, and she lay for a long time before putting out her arms to him, extending, then extending again, the deadline she had set herself for the resumption of the nightmare. *Nothing more can happen until after Henry…*

'Hello, darling! I thought your head… Oh, Olga!'

If they were listening, they would discover at the outset that they were not going to destroy her as a woman.

CHAPTER 4

'Reckon I'd better have a clean-out this morning, Mrs Trent, round about they bushes in the front.'

Jim Riddock pushed his cap to the back of his head and gazed thoughtfully through the kitchen window.

Assailed by panic at the implications of this innocent suggestion, Olga collapsed into a chair and lowered her whirling head to her lap, hoping she might appear to be contemplating a mark on her skirt. But Jim Riddock was still engrossed with the farthest rooftops.

'I suppose it must be a bit overgrown round there, Jim,' she eventually managed. *But please leave it alone.* Sometimes, when she went out on foot, the rustle of weight on dead leaves was too heavy for blackbirds. 'I think, though, it would be better if you concentrated today on the back.' Again she must improvise. 'My husband is rather anxious to get the vegetable garden tidy.' There was no way she could have explained to the KGB that she wasn't trying to flush them out, and no way Henry and Jim Riddock could meet now that Jim Riddock came on a weekday, and wonder between them what had got into Mrs Trent.

'As you say, Mrs T,' responded Jim Riddock reluctantly. 'You're the boss.'

'Well, my husband is, so we'd better do what he wants.' She was able to get up. 'More coffee, Jim?'

'Thanks, Mrs Trent, but I'll get going. Make the most of a decent morning.'

It was hard to believe, thought Olga, yearning after her slowly retreating gardener, that there had once been a time when she had rejoiced to find herself alone. Now, from the moment solitude began, she was listening for the telephone, wanting to fall on the neck of Mrs Metcalfe, Jim Riddock, Pam, the postman, when she saw them at the door, and of course the children...

Less than a week, but already Monday and Friday morning with Mrs Metcalfe were established oases of respite for her straining ears. The other weekday mornings, the early afternoons, were Indian territory through which she crept alert, using housework, television and translations to help herself along. When her students arrived it was hard not to fall on their necks, too, even while it was impossible not to look at them askance. The telephone lost its terrors at the weekend, but one end had been enough to show her the unremitting strains and snares of Saturday and Sunday...

Really, though, she wanted the telephone to ring, wanted to find out precisely what was to happen. Once she was told about the steps she must take, the job she must get, the things she must look for, she would be able to stop her imagination circling above that dim fear she had so far managed not to dredge up from the pit of her subconscious...

She wasn't expecting anyone, and the front doorbell had her heart so unruly she had to press her hands against it as she ran out to the hall. She didn't expect her instructions to be delivered in person, but she was conditioned, now, to over-react.

On the step was a small reassuring figure.

'Pam! Oh, Pam!'

'As the mountain wouldn't come to Mahomet...'

'It was only because of Jim Riddock, and Henry wanting me to tell him this and that.' Yes, she must want to get the next telephone call over, to have refused Pam's suggestion that she go round for coffee. 'But I'm very glad to see you. What happened to the washing-machine man?'

'He actually came when he said he would, half-past nine, so here I am. Only for the length of a coffee, I've loads to do.'

So for the length of a coffee she had no need to strain her ears. It was probably absurd, but she had to believe her instructors were aware of every movement into and out of her house.

'I'm so glad you came, Pam. I've just seen Jim Riddock off to the vegetables.'

Even such an apparent *non sequitur* was something she should train herself to avoid. But the resilience of human nature, thought Olga as she put the kettle on, was an astonishing thing. The small respite of Pam's visit was giving her a moment of comparative cheerfulness.

'You look better,' said Pam, bringing the moment to an end.

'Better than what?' Olga worked on her smile before turning round.

'Well, than you did – when was it? – the day before yesterday. I thought you looked quite washed out then.'

'You didn't say.' Olga crossed the kitchen for a tin of biscuits.

'It would only have made you feel worse if I had. I'm saying now because you look better. Promise me you'll go to the doctor if these headaches persist.'

'I promise. By the way, I've had my invitation from the little lady with the curls. Afternoon tea on Tuesday of next week.'

She really ought to be keeping two diaries, to record her engagements in the two worlds. *Tuesday: Tea with Mavis Heap. Tuesday: Carry out the first of the instructions.*

'You have? And she hasn't given me a second chance! One would have thought it

63

would be the ideal opportunity. Either our Mavis is easily deterred, or she believes in dividing and ruling. There *are* people like that. On the domestic level as well as in business.'

'I suppose so.' Somewhere far off she was aware that Pam's thesis was interesting. Little Mavis Heap must be looking for an ally, and considered it more promising to pursue one neighbour at a time, and especially not two friends together... That was quite good, she had forgotten herself for a full half minute, perhaps she could bring self-discipline to bear in this direction as well, try to give herself the odd break.

'But I don't know, do I, if you accepted? Did you, Olga?'

'Yes. Unfortunately I don't have a pupil on Tuesday, and I couldn't think up another excuse quickly enough.'

'I expect she found out you don't teach on a Tuesday,' said Pam, grinning her ignorance of what she was doing to Olga's heart.

'Perhaps.' Either it was a coincidence, or tea with Mavis Heap, rather than the telephone, was the next step...

'Olga, are you sure you're all right?'

'Just dizzy for a moment. I'm so normal and well most of the time, I know it isn't anything to worry about.'

'You've told Henry?'

'No. And don't *you*, Pam!'

'You know I wouldn't! But I shall go on chivvying you to tell him yourself if it goes on.'

'It's better if I forget it. It never seems to happen when I'm working on a translation, or with a pupil. Psychology.'

'Not altogether, it can't be... Heavens, I must go, I've so much shopping and I'm working this afternoon.'

'Do you enjoy working in your library, Pam? All these years I don't think I've ever asked you.'

'I adore it. I even tend to feelings of regret that by slacking off to part-time I've stopped myself climbing the ladder, especially as I've got quite good qualifications.'

'Sometimes I think I'd like a job again.' She had said it before she knew she was going to, but there was no harm in sounding out reaction.

'You, Olga?' Pam was surprised. 'I thought your students and translations added up to one. To say nothing of being there for Martin and Lucy.'

Olga tried out a laugh. 'I expect I'm just talking off the top of my head.'

As she saw Pam out she wondered if the men in the bushes had radios, to be able to tell their bosses without delay that the coast was clear. The men in the cars surely did. In the past week Olga had glimpsed unfamiliar cars in The Crescent – she had done no more than glance at them as she left the house or came home – and had decided that although the KGB would want to conceal evidence of actual trespass, there was really no reason for them not to let her be aware of surveillance outside her gates. And if challenged by other residents, or local police, they would have their salesmen's goods and papers ready to prove the innocence of their presence...

She was in the kitchen doorway and the telephone was ringing.

Before the nightmare began, I had telephone calls. And, of course, she had had them since. Each one, though, took a toll. She stumbled to the chair beside the telephone.

'Olga Trent here.'

Last week, she had said 'Hello' when she lifted the receiver. This way, she could cut out the first of the cold, clear questions.

'Oh, Mrs Trent, it's Warings the grocers. The Kee Mun tea you ordered ten days ago. It's in at last. I'm sorry you've had so long to wait. Mrs Trent?'

'I'm here, yes. Thank you very much for letting me know. I'll be in Richmond some time tomorrow, I'll collect it then.'

'Very good, Mrs Trent. Thank you. Goodbye, now.'

The young cheerful voice ended on a click, and when Olga had hung up too she stayed where she was, her head against her knees until it cleared. Then when she eventually got up she went quickly back to the kitchen. She would walk down the garden and see how Jim Riddock was doing, she couldn't take another telephone call just yet and all at once she longed to be out under the pale blue autumn sky.

As she reached the back door the front doorbell rang again.

She could ignore it, act as if she was already down the garden. But of course she wouldn't.

This time she walked to Henry's mother's gilt-framed mirror and stared at her frantic, wide-eyed face until it regained a comparative calm. Then opened the door.

On the step, almost hidden by an enormous bunch of variegated flowers, stood Hugo.

'Good morning, Olga. I had an assignment along The Crescent – children and cats, very charming – and I couldn't resist the chance to call on you.'

'Come in, Hugo,' said Olga dazedly, at last moving out of the way. She held out her hands for the flowers before Hugo offered them, then realized as if realizing the bad manners of another woman that she should have let the first gesture be his.

Not that Hugo had noticed, he was talking.

'...especially as Henry had said you

weren't quite yourself.'

As unobtrusively as possible, Olga leaned back against the wall.

'Henry said that?' Henry hadn't said anything to her about how he thought she was since the day of the first telephone call. Except to ask once or twice if the headache was still holding off. Alarm defined the shape of her body, running from her head to her feet and her fingertips. 'When did you see Henry, Hugo?'

'On the train back from town last night. The only time we've coincided on the railway, now I think of it, but I don't keep office hours, darling, as you well know. I'd hoped to avoid the crush, but what with one thing and another in London, I was stuck in the thick of it. Not coping very well, then there was Henry pulling me down beside him into the last available seat. Didn't he tell you?'

'No, but he only had time to wash and change before we were out for dinner. Don't take it personally, Hugo dear.' As she was trying not to take it. 'Will you have coffee or sherry? At eleven-thirty I think either would be perfectly proper.' More and more frequently she found her voice coming to her aid of its own accord. 'Anyway, go and sit down in the sitting-room and think about it while I put these lovely flowers into water.' But she had to ask him then and there. 'What exactly did Henry say about me?'

'I don't know if I can manage to be exact, but I think he said he felt you were under the weather, too much over your books and probably not enough fresh air. Something like that.'

'I see. He's wrong, you know.' Particularly as she had told him of the extra walks she had been taking in Kew Gardens. And he had heard her. 'You seem to have had more walks in a week than you normally have in a month, darling,' he had said. So why had he told Hugo she wasn't getting enough fresh air? 'You don't think I look "under the weather", do you, Hugo?'

Determinedly, Olga smiled at him.

'Under the weather is not a phrase I would apply to *anyone* of my acquaintance,' said Hugo with distaste. 'Sometimes Henry forces me to feel that he is lacking in the niceties.' She had all the attention of the wide brown eyes. 'But you don't look quite as usual, darling. A little spiritual, perhaps. Pale and interesting. That, of course, is not something to be deplored from the aesthetic point of view, but it could I suppose indicate a current lack of robustness. Are you all right, Olga?'

The sudden direct question, accompanied by an equally sudden flood of concern into the appraising eyes, had her seeking the support of the wall for the second time.

'I'm perfectly all right, Hugo! And please

tell Henry so if you bump into him again! Oh, these lovely flowers, I must give them water. Is it to be coffee or sherry?'

'Neither, I regret. I'm already late for a sitting, and although I don't at all mind being considered eccentric, I would deplore a reputation for unreliability. I must leave you, Olga.'

His arms were out and she put the flowers down so that he could embrace her. The fierceness of the brief pressure was a surprise, but not now a worry, and she returned it on a fierce reaction of her own: an intense desire to let Hugo into the nightmare. He was intelligent, he was ingenious, despite his extravagance he kept his counsel…

'Goodbye, Hugo dear. We'll see you soon.'

She watched him into his car and round the curve of the drive before going slowly into the kitchen to find a vase for the flowers. Hugo's account of Henry's somewhat puzzling remark, although it made her uneasy, was an almost welcome dilution of the terror which when she was alone and unoccupied flooded every crevice of her brain. As was the necessity of going down the garden to tell Jim Riddock his lunch was ready.

At least, thought Olga, watching the persistent dew splash up over the toes of her shoes as she left the path to look closer at a delicate blue-grey cluster of autumn crocus, she was learning to marvel at things which before the telephone call she had scarcely noticed. Perhaps because the whole normal world, now, was the other side of the glass bubble which surrounded her, a series of pictures in a gallery seen clearly because objectively. Even Henry, despite the nightly closeness of his flesh...

By half past twelve Jim Riddock had finished his lunch and was edging conversationally through the back door, still reluctant to retrace his steps to the vegetables while the ground round the front gate cried out for his spade and rake. Half an hour later, after her own small snack, Olga crossed the hall on her way to the dining-table and a translation, and saw the envelope on the floor.

It was a strong manila envelope folded over something knobbly and roughly round. Written on the envelope were no more than the two words *Olga Trent*, and there was no stamp. She knew at once that it was stage two.

So all her sick fear of the telephone... It was too late, as well as too unwise, to open the front door and look towards the gate. Olga carried the envelope into the dining-room and set it on the table, having to struggle against hysterical laughter. She left it there while she went for a paper knife, then sat down and very carefully opened it.

The object inside was something it took

her a few minutes to recognize. With it in the envelope was a small piece of paper on which were typed a letter, two numbers, and the one word *Paddington*. Whether the word helped her or not she didn't know, but as she held the weightless device on her hand and stared at the thin protusion of metal under the red plastic handle she saw in her mind's eye the close rows of miniature metal tenements with people opening and closing the small squares into which they were divided, and knew she held the key to a station locker. At Paddington. At a station she and her neighbours would not normally use. As she reached into one particular cube interior she would be unlikely to see Pam, or Jim Riddock, or the little lady with the careful curls.

The envelope held nothing else. Olga put the locker key and the piece of paper back inside it, and the envelope into her handbag, then like a sleepwalker climbed the stairs. They would know, of course, that she had no pupil that afternoon, that Martin was staying on at school until five o'clock because one of his friends was holding a birthday party in the formroom, that Lucy was out to tea.

She would go up to town at once, collect whatever was in the locker, take it to the comfortable anonymity of a large hotel, and absorb it without fear of interruption over the pot of tea she would obviously need, even though whatever she found would only be giving chapter and verse to what she already knew.

Wouldn't it?

Then she would stay there until she had just the right amount of time to catch a train, collect the car, and pick up Martin at five o'clock. She wouldn't need to tell Henry, or anyone else, that she had been to London. He wasn't going to coincide with Jim Riddock, and if he rang and there was no reply, she'd been to the Gardens again...

Olga shrugged off her dismay at the prospect of another lie as she shrugged on her coat. When she was ready she stopped for a second to look again at her face in the mirror, but there was no change she could see beyond a greater prominence of bone. Perhaps that was what Hugo the photographer had meant. She put out some cake and a mug, then ran down the garden to tell Jim Riddock to make himself tea when he was ready, to lock the back door when he left and go out by the front.

The station environs were usually full of cars from the morning rush hour onwards, but Olga slid into a space vacated as she drove up, ridiculing her reaction that even this was being arranged for her, and a train came in as she walked on to the platform.

Turnham Green, Stamford Brook, Ravenscourt Park... She was relaxed enough, for the time being, to remember how strange and beautiful these names had seemed to her as she read them out from the enamel discs on her first tube journey, adding them to the store of wonders which had already begun to make up the mosaic of her new life in England.

At Paddington she had to discipline herself to walk at a normal pace across the concourse. She didn't ask the whereabouts of the lockers, she strolled about until she found them, then cruised the aisles with the memory of the letter and the numbers she had learned on the second train.

The locker was at eye level, one of the smaller ones, and she didn't get the key out until she was standing in front of it. Her hand was shaking so much it took her a few seconds to get the key in, and then to turn it. When the door eventually swung open she could see nothing inside the locker, but her tentative fingers over the edge encountered paper, and she drew out another manila envelope, this time thin and flat.

So no need for her largest handbag, for the carrier bag folded small down the side of it. Olga tucked the envelope in beside the carrier, unable as she turned round to resist a glance to each side of her – the first time she had given in to her perpetual outdoor impulse to turn her head. The elderly woman nearby was, of course, genuinely engaged with a locker, and there was no one else in sight.

Even in the Great Western Hotel she didn't touch the envelope until her tea tray arrived, providing her with a spoon handle to slit it open. When she had poured herself a cup of tea she put her hand into the envelope and slid out its contents – a sheet of typed white A4 paper. The job, thought Olga urgently, as she spread it out, details of the job they would require her to obtain, the beginning of the long haul towards betrayal...

She seemed to read the page at a glance. Then, still careful, she folded the sheet and returned it to the envelope and the envelope to her bag before picking up her cup and burning her mouth on the scalding tea. She set the cup down sharply, but as she leaned back in the low chair, staring across the room, she scarcely felt the discomfort.

It was not, after all, to be a long haul. What she, Olga Lubimova, had to do would be done in a second, and preparation would take a matter of hours.

Gradually she was aware of a face forming out of the mist, a polite, inquiring, slightly anxious face, which she ought to do something about. A savage effort of self-discipline rewarded her with the realization that the face belonged to a woman, alone behind another teapot at the next table. To get rid of the woman's anxiety, to make her turn away, she must smile at her.

Eventually she managed it, and to her astonishment the woman smiled back before turning her attention to the cake on her plate. But then, of course, although Olga must have looked for a moment as if she was going to faint, there could be nothing in her face to reveal her as a potential assassin.

CHAPTER 5

She had only skimmed the sheet of paper, but she knew the gist of it by heart. Preparation for the atrocity was to take place on Tuesday, so she of the careful curls, Mrs Mavis Heap, would be having another afternoon tea invitation turned down. The KGB would no doubt prefer to have chosen a day without an engagement to be cancelled, but even they had to take the odd small chance. She would tell Mavis Heap that a friend from abroad was unexpectedly in London and would Mavis mind. Then she would suggest another day. 'Just to show that there's no ill feeling,' as Henry might have said in one of his jokey moods. Mavis Heap would show disappointment, then rally... Rigid in her armchair in the lounge of the Great Western Hotel, Olga was trying to absorb the horror by diluting it with her vague memory of that odd little lady who was about to be frustrated again, and with the reassuring smiles she must continue offering to the woman at the next table, still regularly glancing up from her cake to see that Olga was all right. *Yes, I'm all right, I'm not going to faint, although I wish I could.*

She had known when she was half way down the page what she was going to find at the foot if it. After the first few lines extolling her early prowess with firearms, she had had to stand away from that deepest, most dreaded fear she had been so assiduously guarding and let it crawl at last to the surface.

Under the influence of a demagogic teacher she had joined the Komsomol, and on an instinct that she would be able to shoot straight she had assigned herself to a course in weapons training. By some involuntary arrangement of her physical self, some natural co-ordination of hand and eye, she had been an instant star recruit. That would have been enough in itself, perhaps, even though, under the discreet persuasion of her parents, she had not on leaving school transferred her Komsomol membership to membership of the Party. (And her parents had not, for the sake of her burgeoning career, allowed her grandmother – Olga still thought of her as *babushka* – to take her out of Moscow on Sundays to the church of the Novadivici.)

Yes, that might have been enough, but on one of her long introspective weekend walks about the vast spaces of the capital – she knew now why since the telephone call her mind had veered away from what had been her best memory of life in Moscow – she had been threatened by one of the rarer dangers of the Russian capital: a would-be mugger or rapist. She didn't know which he had intended to be, because before he could do more than put his hand on her arm she had brought into play the other skill she had learned in the Komsomol, self-defence. A policeman hurrying to the scene (a few seconds earlier Olga had believed herself to be the only figure in the landscape) saw her cast the villain from her as if he had been a rag doll.

She had gone by the book, but the man had fallen awkwardly and had still been limp when he was carried away. Perhaps he had died – Olga at last permitted the memory of the first time she had thought of herself as a killer – perhaps he had been put to death. She didn't know.

So far as she was concerned it had been praise and glory. She wasn't a Party member but she had learned her skills in the Komsomol and could at least be considered a credit to Mother Russia. She wasn't quite a heroine of the Soviet Union, but for a few days she was well known in Moscow.

But that was six years before Henry arrived for an international congress of civil engineers and she was assigned to work for him. Six years in which her exploits had sunk out of the current consciousness. But not, of course, out of the files of the KGB.

She had been naïve not to realize, from the moment she was asked to sign the condition of her release to the West, what her destiny would ultimately be. But perhaps her instinct had known that such a realization could not have been lived with.

She was living with it now. Sitting in the lounge of the Great Western Hotel she was facing a choice between killing an unknown victim and condemning her two children to death. Or worse. And trying not to look at the third possibility...

The woman at the next table had finished her cake and was wiping her lips. She smiled at Olga again over the paper serviette.

At least there would be no telephone call between now and Tuesday. But there would be a weekend. There would be Henry and Martin and Lucy, the one observing and making her wary, the others demanding and making her tired. All she wanted to do, now, was to curl up small and silent and alone...

Perhaps she had lost her old skill. Perhaps she could pretend she had. If there was a chance of her being unreliable through no fault of her own, they would hardly insist on her carrying out her assignment.

I need hardly remind you that you have two young children.

She would have to hurry if she wanted to pick Martin up at five.

'Excuse me... Oh, forgive me, I didn't

mean to startle you.'

The woman from the next table had stopped beside her and spoken, and she had brought out that little moaning sound.

'I'm sorry, I was miles away.'

'I just wanted...' said the woman awkwardly. 'When you came in I didn't think you looked very well. Are you all right?'

'Thank you, yes. I had a headache and the aspirins seem to have worked.' Shuddering at her choice of lie, Olga got to her feet. At least the smiles had staved this off until they were both leaving. 'It is most kind of you to bother.' She heard her voice more Russian, less English.

'Not at all. Well, I'll be on my way.' Smiling now with embarrassment, the woman walked quickly ahead to indicate that their association was at an end.

Olga was ten minutes late at the school, but the party was still in full swing and it was a quarter to six when she and Martin arrived at Sadie's to collect Lucy.

Leaving his party before he was ready made Martin rather tiresomely lively, and it was harder than it had been a week ago not to over-react to his restless movements about the car. Although she could never again be glad of anything, Olga was glad when they got home. Glad, too, that she would have Friday to indulge her numbness before the continuous demands of the weekend.

'You don't look too well again, Olga,' said Henry in the hall, at the end of his scrutiny. So from the edge of the abyss to the bottom had left a further mark.

'I haven't felt very well today.' She had an inspiration. 'I suspect I'm starting an early menopause.'

'At thirty-seven?' He had raised one eyebrow, signal of scepticism.

'Women vary.' She heard annoyance in her voice. 'I know I'm not ill. But then I'm suddenly dizzy. Suddenly hot and cold. Suddenly – a bit bothered.' It would be as well to cover her manner and the expression of her face as well. 'It doesn't worry me, Henry, I don't want to make a thing of it. I really don't want to talk about it, and certainly not outside the house. Hugo called this morning with an enormous bunch of flowers, as if for an invalid. Apparently you told him on the train that I was under the weather. But you didn't even tell me that you had seen him.'

'Oh, Olga.' Henry hugged her, for once at a loss, and despite herself she was briefly comforted. 'With dashing out last night I completely forgot. And I just happened to be thinking about you, and that you didn't seem to be quite yourself, when I saw Hugo on the train. I'm sorry, I wasn't telling tales, darling. Put it down to the anxieties of a fond and foolish husband.'

'It's all right. The flowers are lovely, come

and see.'

By destroying those parts of her life which were separate from the nightmare she would not make the nightmare any less. (Nothing would do that.) So she would be stubborn, she would resist its total encroachment, she would keep what she could.

She would keep this beginning to a normal evening.

'Aren't they lovely?' she said, indicating the large brilliant bowl as Henry walked across to the drinks cupboard.

'Typical Hugo,' said Henry. 'But yes, they are very splendid. Whisky?'

'A large one.' Olga sank down on to the sofa. 'The children have both had special days. I'll let them tell you.' Because it was too much effort, and she didn't want to surface from the new somnolence which seemed to have settled over her. 'Thank you, darling.' She took the cold glass from his long slim hand. The first thing she had noticed about Henry when she had drawn an official chair up beside him had been his hands on the table, loosely holding a sheaf of papers, and five minutes after taking her seat she had wanted them to touch her.

'What are you thinking about?' he asked now.

'I was thinking about the day we met. Your hands.'

But that thought was being swallowed by

the thought that if she had no alternative to killing someone, the person she killed ought to be herself. Treason or suicide was enough of a moral dilemma. Murder or suicide surely permitted only one decision…

She couldn't unlock her smile, which by now must be a rictus. But Henry, after murmuring, 'Ah, that day,' had mercifully turned away.

'I'll look in on Martin,' said Olga. 'He was so excited after the party he may not have settled down to his prep.' Five minutes earlier she had been determined to keep this early evening time inviolate, but she was on her feet again.

'You seem a little excited yourself, Olga. Do sit down for a moment longer.'

'Yes, of course… I'm sorry, Henry.'

'Perhaps you need a tonic,' said Henry. 'I can't think you'd be imagining menopausal symptoms at your age if you weren't a bit run down.'

'I'm not imagining them.' *Your first assignment.* She must get the idea across to Henry, she would need it a long way beyond next Tuesday. If, of course, she decided to remain alive. But how long could she keep on surpassing one supreme effort with another? 'But they're nothing to worry about. The thing to do is to try and think of other things. I'm always all right when I'm working, so I ought to be all right when I'm playing. What about asking Pam if she can come in on Saturday night, and taking me out to dinner?' *Nothing more can happen until after Henry and I...* And if it was to be her last weekend she would prefer to enjoy it.

'That would be wonderful.' But he was sitting forward on the sofa and searching her face.

Pam was free and enthusiastic, and Henry booked a table at their favourite local restaurant.

The temporary bulwark helped Olga through Friday, and she decided while having coffee with Mrs Metcalfe that she would wait until the experience of Tuesday was behind her before assembling the sedatives.

Am I really considering my death? she asked herself at her bedroom window when Mrs Metcalfe had gone, and found no answer while there was still a strand of foolish hope, while she still might be able to persuade them she had lost her nerve and her skill...

It was as unbelievable as anything else about the nightmare that she really was able to enjoy Saturday night. By wearing the evening like a stole round her shoulders, as protection against the cold to come.

They danced to a three-piece band, and reminisced about the best moments of their marriage and friendship. It was her farewell party, which she had arranged, and she was making the most of its every moment. The valedictory glow was so dazzling, Olga almost forgot now and then that Henry wasn't aware of it.

Drinking rather more than usual helped her sustain the illusion even when they were on the way home. As did Henry's own rather untypical lightness of mood. When they got out of the car she was even giggling and Henry was whispering rude witticisms in her ear.

'Hi Pam!' she called cheerfully, as she and Henry, entwined, stumbled towards the step where Pam was standing.

'Well, really!' said Pam, staring from one to the other.

'We're drunk,' said Olga, having no difficulty in smiling.

'No, we're not,' said Henry, so coldly Olga drew away from him. 'If we were – if I was – we'd have taken a taxi.'

'All right, darling,' said Olga, too loudly in her sudden frantic desire to maintain a vestige of her comparative light-heartedness. 'Only a joke.'

'I'm sorry.' Henry took her hand as they went into the house.

'Of course I wouldn't have believed you were drunk, Henry, at the wheel of your car,' said Pam, grinning. 'But for Olga it could have been fun.' Pam winked at her as Henry bent to stroke the cat.

'Well, I think I am, a little. But it's reached the stage where I want some tea. Will you join us, Pam?' All at once she didn't feel anything, beyond a desire to sleep. It was a relief that Pam shook her head.

'Better get back to Brian. Really, Henry, there's no need to come with me.'

'But you know I will.' Henry turned to Olga. 'Tea for two, please, darling.' He had half resumed his jokey manner, but there was something in his eyes, when they briefly met Olga's, which she was unable to read, and she gave an involuntary shiver.

'Cold?' Henry's expression, now, was all concern.

'No. Just the goose on the grave. You know, that is an English idiom I have only just learned. From one of my students.'

'You sound rather Russian tonight,' said Henry.

'Because she's drunk,' said Pam.

Olga had the strange sensation that if she waved her arms about she could send them both – and the cat, and the house, and the Crescent – flying in all directions like a pack of cards. But that, of course, was only possible in sleeping nightmares. And brought them to an end.

'Good night, Pam, thank you so much. We had a lovely time.'

'Good night, dear heart!'

When Henry got back his jokey manner

had disappeared again and as he sat down opposite her at the kitchen table and picked up his mug of tea he seemed sunk in thought.

'Is there anything, Henry?'

'What's that, darling?' His eyes focused on her slowly. For the first time since the telephone call, her face, her voice, her manner were not his chief concern. But somehow she wasn't reassured.

'Is anything worrying you?'

'Of course not.' There came the heart-stopping smile. 'It was a good evening.'

'Yes. I shall always remember it.'

In bed, unusually, Henry did not wait for her invitation. Already guilt-ridden, she might not have been able to offer it, and she moved gratefully into his arms, glad of his modest preference for love in the dark, with the freedom it brought her face to express despair as well as ecstasy.

Her farewell continued as successfully on Sunday. The weather was calm and blue and gold and they spent most of the day in the garden, the children tending their own small plots of ground – Lucy steadily meticulous, Martin in sudden destructive bursts – or playing on the rough grass of the glade and cheerfully carting wheelbarrow loads of weeds and dead shoots to the rubbish tip.

When Henry thanked her for a special weekend, Olga had the small satisfaction of knowing she would at least be leaving her affairs in order.

Monday passed like a dream. She was so far, now, from her old life – poised in no man's land on her way to the new one – it had grown almost easy to act it out, to rely on the reflexes assembled over her decade as Mrs Olga Trent. Her request for understanding from Mavis Heap was so reasonable, so concerned, the lady was scarcely disturbed and purred contentedly off the telephone on the promise of a very short delay.

'Isn't it tomorrow you're having tea with a strange lady in Ardley Grove?' asked Henry in bed on Monday night.

'I meant to tell you... D'you remember Ailsa Williams?' Ailsa Williams had emigrated with her husband to New Zealand, and about three years ago the exchange of Christmas cards had ceased.

'Vaguely.' In the new nocturnal pattern which seemed to be taking shape Henry was already drawing her against him.

'She and her husband went to New Zealand. She rang today, she's in London briefly and wants me to go up for lunch. The little lady in Ardley Grove was very understanding–'

'Go up for lunch, darling,' murmured Henry. 'So long as you come home for dinner.'

By then her shudder was ambiguous.

They had known, of course, that she was not doing the school run on Tuesday afternoon. But as the children had no after-school activities, they would see to it that she was home by four. That was no doubt why they wanted her outside Kew Gardens station at half past nine in the morning. This time, as a car slid out of a parking space in front of her, Olga did not ridicule her instinctive belief that the space had been reserved for her.

A back door of the car parked close on the right was already open. She was inside, and the door shut, without seeing more of the two people in the front, and the one who followed her into the back, than that they were men. Before she could turn her head, be aware of anything but the darkened windows, soft cloth was over her eyes and secured behind.

'We are sorry, Olga Lubimova.' The voice spoke English even more precisely than she did. 'It is a precaution that you will appreciate.'

'I appreciate none of this.' *I need hardly remind you that you have two young children.* 'But yes, I understand, of course.'

There was no response, and the men did not speak among themselves. The car held a sour, sharp smell of tobacco, but she thought it was from impregnated clothes and fittings rather than actual smoke. The driver swung it jerkily round and back, made a noisy gear-change, and roared away. Olga had hoped she might at least recognize the direction in which they started off, but she was instantly lost.

She could monitor time, though, if not place. By dint of assiduous counting – seconds in her mind, minutes on her fingers – she reckoned that when they eventually came to a stop their erratic driver had been at the wheel for just under half an hour.

'I will help you out.'

The same voice, from beside her.

'Thank you.'

Fresh air. Another indignant blackbird. No other sounds beyond the shuffling of her own feet, being guided across gravel and then up one, two steps.

A key in a lock, a muffled curse and then her feet were on carpet, she was being walked across what must be a good-sized hall. Another door creaked open ahead of her.

'Steps,' said the only voice which had yet spoken. 'Downstairs.'

A sudden giddiness, as her tentative foot found the lower hold. These steps, like the steps outside, seemed to be made of stone. She counted twelve of them.

'It is flat now.' She was guided a little way forward, on a cold floor. 'Please sit down here.'

The hard chair was immediately behind her when she put her hand back. As she took it her arm was released, leaving her in a panic of disorientation.

'Please...' she gasped.

Now she herself was no longer moving, she could hear the heavy feet on the floor.

'It is all right, Olga Lubimova.' The voice, at a slight remove, was for the first time tinged with reassurance. 'Please sit where you are, and in a moment you will be able to take off the blindfold.'

The footsteps now were back by the stairs, were climbing them. When they had receded almost out of earshot a door closed. Olga sat in total silence and darkness, her hands pressed between her knees to prevent them tearing at the band across her eyes. She couldn't count seconds any more, and had no idea how many minutes had passed when a voice spoke again. Perhaps the same voice, but it was impossible to be certain because it came at her distorted from every direction as it told her to remove the blindfold.

Her fingers were too clumsy to undo the knot and she pulled the cloth roughly up over her hair, blinking from the dazzle of the unshaded overhead light bulbs. The cellar was large, much longer than its width, empty but for the chair where she sat and the table beside it, the loudspeaker, and the television eye on each side of the longer walls. And something regularly black and white at the far end.

'All right, Olga Lubimova.' The voice filled the space. 'Take your time, but when you are ready, please begin to practise.'

Olga was on her feet from the shock of the voice, and walked slowly towards those black and white motifs on the far short wall. She was half way there, stumbling on the uneven floor, when she realized what they were. Four effigies of men in a row, their hearts and heads defined by white circles fading to grey.

Olga stood looking at them, endowing them in her mind with bodies and blood, then turned and walked like a zombie back to the chair and the table. On the table, beside some more sheets of A4 paper and a Thermos flask, were a box of ammunition and a gun.

CHAPTER 6

The gun was of a type she had handled before, although never with a silencer. (Was the silencer to protect her ears and the anonymity of the house under which she was imprisoned, or to simulate ultimate conditions?) Appalled by the instant familiarity of the procedure across the years of her life in England, Olga loaded, then advanced to the firing line indicated on the rough floor. Her hand trembled so violently that when, still a zombie, she attempted to hit one of those round white discs, the bullet went wide of the whole target. Her next attempt hit a foot... She wasn't a zombie, she was a human being about to take the last chance of escape.

Her arm now was settling down, she knew that the third time she sought the target she would find it. Showing herself to be taking time and care to set the shot up, in the second before firing Olga turned the muzzle of the gun the fraction from the white centre which was all that was needed to send her shot into a dummy hand. At the same time she was aware of the forgotten sensation of hope. Her very skill could help her to be convincingly unskilful…

'You can do better than that, Olga Lubi-mova.'

Hope was a cold shock in the pit of her stomach. But she had been a fool, they must have her in close-up, they would have seen that final minute deviation. The thing to do was to aim a fraction awry from the start. That way she would offer them no proof that she wasn't trying.

The next shot hit an upper leg. The one after that, an arm.

'You are wasting time, Olga Lubimova.' The walls, the ceiling, accused her, with no more expression than the telephone. 'Your eyesight has not deteriorated. You are still capable of hitting your target. Perhaps it will help you to be reminded that you have two young children. You may sit down for a moment. No, you will not read until you have successfully practised.'

She had scarcely realized that she had picked up the papers. Dropping them back on to the table as if they were suddenly redhot, Olga sat with her head down and her eyes closed, her hands gripped again between her knees.

This is happening. I have to accept it. And that while I am here I must do as I am told. When I am free once more, at home, perhaps… But not now.

Olga picked up the gun again, advanced to

the firing line, took aim and pierced a heart. Then went back to the table and reloaded. Of the next six bullets, only one failed to find the centre of a circle. Her emotions, while she fired, were frozen into non-existence. Was that how contract killers...? But they chose to do their job, she was of course no nearer to understanding them.

'An admirable performance, Olga Lubimova.' She was back at the table, about to load again. 'We suggest, now, that you sit down and read the papers on the table before continuing with your practice. You of course brought with you the sheet you have already received, you would not at any time have left it away from your person. You will see that on the table beside you there is also some blank paper and a pen. When you have read the new paper please write down on the blank sheets the things vital for you to remember, in the form of notes which will make sense only to you. You will, of course, guard the notes as carefully as you have guarded the paper you received, but should they fall into other hands their form must assure that they do not appear to be significant. You will leave all the other papers on the table. We will look at your notes before you leave, to make sure you have understood our intentions. You may drink coffee while you read.'

The voice left an echo, which had to die

away before the absolute silence resumed. When it had settled back Olga turned her chair to the table and reluctantly lowered her eyes, holding them carefully averted from the papers. She unscrewed the plastic cup from the flask top and filled it with the steaming liquid from the flask, raising it at once to her lips. It had the right taste as well as the right colour, and was free of sugar. But they would know, of course, how Olga Lubimova liked her coffee. When she had drained the cup and filled it again she set it down on the table, so ringed and discoloured with stains her instinctive gesture of wiping the underside of the cup filled her with self-scorn. Then she picked up the papers.

She had two weeks to the day in which to carry out her assignment. She could choose her own time, but her choice would obviously be influenced by the account of the habits and movements of her subject as set out below...

'Olga Lubimova, you are not reading constructively, you are not preparing to take notes.'

Her shock and despair must be showing on the monitor, proclaiming themselves in every drooping line of her body. The effort with which she pulled herself upright and drew pen and paper towards her was more arduous than anything that the nightmare had so far demanded. Underneath the blank paper was the page already sent to her which she had been carrying in her handbag. Her handbag... The woman who forgot her handbag was a woman in a void. She had not been aware of hers since the blindfold had covered her eyes, but she had not been aware, either, that she was without it. They had picked it up in the car and extracted the paper, and the man who had brought her to the cellar had slipped the paper on to the table...

There was nothing in that first sheet, really, that she needed in writing. She knew her own history, and she knew the nature of her assignment. From the new papers she made slow, painfully formed words on a blank sheet, forcing her hand along as if recovering from a stroke. Name. (She wrote the three elements of the name in different places on the paper.) Physical description. Personal habits. Her own preparations (which must take place immediately before she carried out the assignment). Disconnected key words which would act as catalyst to her outraged memory. Not that she needed even those, everything that happened in the nightmare she knew by heart, had always known. But they had told her to take notes, they were going to read them, and her memory could go the other way, from unnaturally sharp to a dimness of breakdown...

Feeling was more than frozen, it had been

cut off, tied up like a severed umbilical cord. Olga read what she had written critically and objectively, and knew it to be the precise requirement. Then she set it on the table next to the little pile of papers she would not be taking with her, drained the third and final cup of coffee, and sat back against the wooden slats of the chair to wait. Hoping not to wait long, not to be given time to discover, while still in this impossible place, that after all her emotions were merely in abeyance...

'It appears that you have completed your task with the papers, Olga Lubimova. Good. And you have finished your coffee. Please load the gun again and recommence your practise.'

This time she did her best from the start. Of the six bullets, only one failed to find the exact centre of her target.

'That is excellent, Olga Lubimova. But we notice you aim always for the heart. Please now load six more bullets and aim in each case for the head, which in certain circumstances could be the only part of the target available.'

In certain circumstances... Available... Suddenly she felt physically sick and had to swallow savagely in order not to retch echoingly about the cellar. She had hoped that her emotions had perished, but she was still seeing the targets as bodies with bones and blood. With faces. And now, with one particular face…

Nevertheless, of course, Olga obediently reloaded and shot six times at a representative head. Each bullet found the white centre of the target.

'That is satisfactory, Olga Lubimova, highly satisfactory.'There was still no expression in the pervasive voice. 'So satisfactory it is clear that the practice need continue no longer. Please sit down and replace the blindfold across your eyes. We can see whether or not you do this effectively.'

Whether or not I cheat.

Olga's hands, which had been so steady with the gun in them, fumbled for several seconds with the knot in the silk scarf, and took even longer to tie it again at the back of her head. When she was certain she could see nothing she raised her face and turned it from side to side.

The door at the top of the cellar steps opened almost immediately, and the heavy steps crescendoed towards her. Although she had never been so sure of anything as the inevitability of the hand once more on her arm, she moaned as it touched her.

'Sit still, Olga Lubimova.' The voice as well was back at her side.

The slight scraping sound from the table beside her was followed by the rustle of paper. Then silence.

100

'That is admirable, Olga Lubimova.'

She heard the click of a clasp. They had put the approved notes into her handbag.

'Please get up now.'

The arm led her across the floor, told her when to raise her foot. This time the steps failed to disorientate her, she was expecting them to climb. The carpeted space felt hot and dry, and then she was blessedly in the air again, a breeze tapping her cheek below the blindfold.

She thought it was the same insensitive driver. The count of minutes and seconds produced the same total, too. If she was ever in a position to talk to the police, a twenty-five-minute circle round Kew Gardens tube station would be some help... False hope, insanely optimistic scenarios, must be suppressed as savagely as emotions, the pain of their unreality took too great a toll of her strength.

The car had stopped, someone was getting out of the front passenger seat. Then in again, slamming the door. The blindfold fell away as the back door opened beside her. At the bidding of a gentle pressure she had stumbled out. By the time she was upright and had realized she was standing by her own car door, that her bunch of keys was hanging from the ignition and her handbag was on the passenger seat, the car which had returned her had backed out from the adjoining space and was roaring away, was already too far off for her to read the number plate, turning a corner before she could see more than that it was large and dark.

The new piece of paper had taken the place of the old, tucked neatly down the side of her bag. Sole evidence of how she had spent the morning.

The morning? For the only time since her childhood Olga was without any sense of the time of day, and was seized with panic at the thought of the children waiting on the step which even as it suffused her was relieved by the realization that the KGB would not slip up on one small detail.

Her watch told her it was a quarter to one. For a few moments she was tempted to get out of the car again and take a train to town. Change to the Piccadilly Line at Hammersmith and go on to Green Park and a small exquisite lunch at Fortnum and Mason…

Was she so brutalized, already, to be able to think longingly of a piece of trivial self-indulgence when she had just learned she was to bring a life to an end? But even the law had recognized, not so every long ago, the comfort to a condemned man of a last decent meal.

She had not decided yet, who was to die, but after all she would not go to London, she would go home and leave the car, greet the cat, then walk in the Gardens.

She wouldn't think about what was to be done until after the children were safely home, until after Henry...

She had said her goodbyes, she didn't want another fortnight. When the three of them had gone next morning – although she no longer had hope, Olga still saw them off with her usual cheerful reference to their return – she went carefully round the house collecting all the aspirin and paracetemol-based preparations she could find. A kitchen cupboard, the cupboard in the cloakroom, the medicine chest in the bathroom, a dressing-table drawer, her handbag, an old jacket of Henry's, yielded a haul which was probably lethal, but she would buy a few more packets to be on the safe side.

And even then, even though, with no Mrs Metcalfe, and Sadie Porteous on the school run, this was as good a day as any, she would still not be sure she was going to use them...

Not be sure of anything, because all at once, standing by her bed with her back to the window and the garden, that oblivion which was the one thing she could realis-tically yearn for seemed to be approaching of its own accord. She just had time to throw herself on to the bed, be aware of the packets and bottles bouncing around her, before the blessed darkness closed in.

When she came back, all Olga knew at first

was that she had been away. She lay as she had fallen, diagonally across the bed, her head turned to look out at the sky and the tree-tops as she had looked the day the nightmare had begun. Now the sky was in several shades of grey and seemed very close. Within her field of vision was the bed-side clock, and it told her that her absence had lasted for no more than minutes. But it had left her mind clearer than it had been for weeks, a great, clear, washed space waiting to entertain ideas without panic, telling her within a few more minutes what she must do. And that she was not yet ready to die.

With something of her old decisiveness, Olga sat up and seized the telephone. She might not get hold of Hugo this first time of trying, but she knew from his own statements that he made a point of reserving himself a lunch-hour, at work if not at home. And he was so much better than his partner with the public, he almost always answered the telephone. If he didn't, she would silently replace the receiver and try again later.

'Delaunay Studios. Can we help you?'

'Hugo!' *Oh, Hugo!* 'It's Olga.'

'Olga, my dear, what a lovely surprise! Are you coming to have lunch with me?'

Why not? 'If you're having it at home, Hugo.' Desperately, for the sake of any other listeners, she tried to sound casual. 'I'm not in the mood for eating on show today.'

'Home it shall be, that was my idea anyway. You're all right, are you, Olga?'

In her mind's eye she saw the bright brown eyes suddenly grave, as she had seen them the last night of her livable life, and the goose she had so lately learned about walked again over her grave. 'Of course I am, Hugo,' she said briskly. 'I just felt, not for the first time, that it would be fun to see you.' Perhaps they would wonder if there was something in her life they had missed. 'And I thought it was time you had your book back.' Henry hadn't read it, but she didn't think he was going to.

'Oh, that. But it will be fun, Olga.' Thank goodness he hadn't shown surprise that after seven or eight years of friendship she had for the first time got in touch with him for no real reason in the middle of the day. 'One o'clock? I should be home by half past twelve and you know very well, Olga, that I must have a little time for preparation, even when it is only pâté and fresh bread. I shall pick up the bread on the way home. I was going to anyway. I'll see you at one, my dear friend.'

Dear friend. Oh, please...

'Thank you, Hugo.'

Olga replaced the receiver and jumped off the bed on an instant, found a plastic bag in a bottom drawer, swept the bottles and packets into it, and snuggled the bulbous load down into the drawer so that it would just close. Then looked at her watch. Still only ten-thirty, she would walk in the Gardens. It was damp and dull and windy, normally she would not choose to walk on such a day, but it would be the best way to deal with the waiting hours. *And no need to think about what has to happen until after I have seen Hugo...*

Outside, she welcomed the wind in her hair, the moist sting on her cheek, even her intermittent awareness that the jacket she had chosen was not quite warm enough.

'You're a hardy one today, me dear!'

The little man with the moustache, again. One of the vast army of the innocent against whom they and she were arrayed.

'I just wanted some air.'

'Of course, me dear. You enjoy it!'

On her way to the lake Olga passed only two other people. An old man huddled on a seat, a weatherbeaten woman striding towards a gate. As she strode, herself, she was more aware than she had ever been of the healthy obedience of her limbs, the sensation of rhythm and strength in her movements. Nature had fitted her for a long life.

Out on the open edges the wind was wetter, stronger, she had to struggle against it. If she had brought the plastic bag with her she could have taken the pills and just lain down among the trees and stayed there until it was over...

But they would not, of course, have given her enough time.

Back at home, Olga repaired her hair with a sort of automatic meticulousness. Then her face, putting on a little more make-up than usual. Finally she took Hugo's book from the bottom of the small pile beside Henry's side of the bed, locked up the house, and went out to the car.

She was a zombie again, part of the mechanism of the car as it made its way towards Hugo, arrived, parked itself, close but unobvious, just round the corner. Part of the mechanism of the lift as it silently ascended. Then somehow managing on its own as it moved slowly and steadily along the wide carpeted corridor.

In Hugo's sitting-room it was very quiet. Olga didn't know how long she had crouched there in the quietness, insanely waiting for Hugo to leap to his feet from his unnatural position on the beautiful Tabriz carpet, and beg her forgiveness for so cruel a charade.

She wanted to tell him to get up but she had lost her voice.

At first there had been an echo in her ears, from the screams she had heard – the screams she must have screamed – after

107

pushing open the unlatched front door and calling him and not getting an answer and finding him lying distorted on the sitting-room floor.

Since the echo of the screams had died away there had been no sounds beyond the steady tick of the marble mantel clock and her own sobbing breath.

'Hugo! Please... Hugo!'

At last the words had come out. And at last she was accepting that there would be no response.

Olga dragged herself painfully to her feet and over again to the body, aware that pale sunlight had oozed through a ragged rift in the clouds and was illuminating one of the grotesquely sprawled legs. There were a few drops of blood on that exquisite, expensive carpet.

It was all the blood there was, apart from the red rim to the neat hole in the centre left of Hugo's lilac shirt. He lay on his back, his arms out, palms up as if pleading, his hair fanned out round his head like the hair of a girl. His brown eyes were wide open, neither amused or grave as they stared in astonishment at the ceiling. His tiny, delicately decorated revolver was on the floor, too far away for him to have fired the shot which had killed him. And anyway, there were no powder marks round the small red-rimmed hole.

'Hugo. Oh, Hugo!'

In the silence the clock ticked loudly, reminding her of passing time and that she had none to waste. She couldn't help Hugo but she should be helping herself, eliminating the evidences of her innocent visit, getting inconspicuously away. The quality of the building and the rich curtains and carpets had been effective silencers, but sooner or later someone would come.

She had been a zombie when she arrived and she was a zombie now, slowly and carefully crossing the room, the hall, shutting the front door, coming back into the sitting-room, finding her handbag half under a chair and taking out her handkerchief as if in slow motion. Then bending down for the gun, wiping it because moments or years ago she had touched it, returning it to the place where it had been lying. Then looking carefully round the room before retracing her steps to the front door, wiping door-knobs and door frames as she went.

Olga worked mindlessly and conscientiously, and when she was confident she had left no trace she picked up her jacket from the floor, retrieved the book she had brought back to Hugo without touching the table top where it was lying, slung the strap of her bag over her shoulder, and went for the third time to the front door.

She had her handkerchief out to the latch

when she came back to herself. She let her arm fall to her side and stood stock-still.

'Hugo. Oh, Hugo!'

She had come to ask his help, and he was lying there waiting to give it to her in a way he could never have given it if he had been alive.

If she was in custody charged with murder they would be unable to manipulate her.

If she was in prison there would be no advantage for them in threatening the children.

Olga stuffed her handkerchief back into her bag, caressed the doorknob with her bare hand, then walked swiftly back across the hall, touching things as she went.

In the sitting-room she returned the book to the table, drawing her fingertips across the glass top, threw her jacket down on the sofa with her bag. Then picked up the gun again, caressing this, too, before returning it to the floor.

On the low table near where she had put the book was the sherry glass half full of the sherry Hugo had been drinking. When she went through to the kitchen – the long loaf of bread was still in its flimsy wrapper on the scrubbed table – she found the matching glass upside down on the draining-board and dried it and took it back into the sitting-room, cradling it in her hands. Then crossed the room to Hugo's drinks cupboard and poured a splash of sherry into the glass before setting it down on the table beside the other one.

'Forgive me, Hugo,' she whispered, as for the last time she looked round the room, then went to the telephone and dialled the three nines.

'Which service, please?'

'Police.'

When the police answered she gave her name, and Hugo's name and address.

'And what is the trouble, madam?'

'The trouble is that I have just killed Mr Stratton. I will wait here in his flat for you to come for me.'

Part Two

CHAPTER 7

When Olga let the two uniformed men into Hugo's flat she had her jacket on ready to leave and her bag over her shoulder, but of course it was some time before they took her away. They peered warily past her as she stood aside, as if expecting a booby-trap, and advanced very slowly into the sitting-room, indicating that she should walk between them. She went back, then, to her usual chair.

'Jesus wept!' said the younger of the two, earning one sharp word of reprimand from his senior officer.

'Sorry, Governor. But I mean to say... Shall I telephone?'

'Yes. With gloves on.'

'I rang you from this telephone,' said Olga. 'There's another in the bedroom.' The younger man shot her a glance. 'Yes, I've been in there,' she said wearily, 'to leave my coat when my husband and I have been for dinner.'

'Your husband didn't come with you to-day, though?' inquired the senior officer as the junior, turning his back on the body, gingerly broached the telephone. Olga noticed the effort with which the older man looked towards Hugo.

'No. I called in to return a book Mr Stratton had lent him. There on the table. Not that I needed an excuse. Mr Stratton has been the friend of both of us for a long time.' She took a deep breath. 'That's why it was such a shock when he–'

'Save it, lady, for the CID. It'll be painful for you, so no need to go through it more times than strictly necessary.' The senior man, stiff-kneed with reluctance, had knelt down beside Hugo.

'Thank you,' said Olga, aware of a faint, fleet warmth of gratitude. She turned to sit straight in her chair, so as not to be able to see Hugo. Hugo's *body*, Hugo she would never see again. Suddenly she was struggling to clamp down on the wave of horror which threatened to engulf her indifference.

The younger of the two uniformed men had come off the telephone and the two of them were walking uneasily about the room, not touching anything, making sorties from time to time out to the hall, and presumably into the other areas of the flat. When the doctor arrived the junior policeman took Olga into the kitchen, and stayed there with her, not speaking. The second time the doorbell rang she heard several people come in and go at once to the sitting-room, and after a few minutes two men in plain clothes came into the kitchen, introduced themselves as a detective-inspector and a sergeant, and asked her to go with them to the police station.

'Of course.'

Once she was at the station, months and perhaps years would pass before she could do anything again of her own free will. And then the children...

The children. She wouldn't be there when they got back from school, she would have to contact Henry so that he could get home in time to let them in.

'Are you all right, Mrs Trent?'

'I'm all right, yes, but please may I telephone my husband? I have children who will be coming home from school.'

'Of course, your husband will be contacted for you from the station. Now, Mrs Trent, if you're ready.'

They told her, when she asked again on arrival at what she heard them call sub-divisional headquarters, that they would get in touch with her husband while she was answering questions and giving her statement, and when she had finished the statement, had read it and signed it, Henry was shown into the interview room.

'Please tell me what you've just told the police,' said Henry, ashen-faced, burning-eyed, but as calm as ever as he took her in his arms. There was a policewoman in the room, sitting unobtrusively near the wall, not appearing to be aware of them.

'I thought I would take that book back to Hugo, the one he lent you the last time we had dinner with him.' She too was calm, as calm for once as Henry himself. 'I chose lunch-time because I knew he would invite me to share whatever delicacy–'

'How did you know he would be lunching at home?'

The question came at her more sharply than any of the questions asked so far by the police.

'I rang him, Henry, at the studio.'

Henry blinked rapidly a number of times, sign of his sense that things were serious. 'Of course, darling. I'm sorry, it's just that I can't believe that you–'

'That I killed Hugo.' She stared at him, forcing his horrified eyes to hold her gaze. 'I'll tell you about.' She knew the WPC had begun to strain her ears, from the tense way she was now sitting. 'Hugo poured us each a sherry. It was while we were drinking it, when I'd only been there a short time, a few minutes. Hugo suddenly – came at me. Henry, it was as if he had a brainstorm, perhaps didn't even realize any more that it was me. I was standing just beside the chest of drawers where he keeps that little gun

from his shooting club days which he likes –
liked – to show off with. I only had to put
my hand out and pull the drawer open,
glance down... When I got the gun out and
pointed it at him I didn't mean to shoot. You
know my confidence with firearms... I took
the safety-catch off to frighten him, bring
him back to himself, but he still came on...
At the back of my mind I didn't believe that
the gun would be loaded, perhaps that is
why I wasn't absolutely careful with the
trigger. I don't think even so I meant to pull
it, but the gun is so light. I was shocked
when it went off, the sound seemed to come
from somewhere else... It will be manslaughter, won't it, Henry? I took the gun in
self-defence. But of course I shall be
remanded in custody, I shan't be given bail.'

'I think you're still shocked, my darling.
Not realizing... It isn't manslaughter, or any
other charge, as yet, Olga.'

'Not yet, no, but it must be, Henry, I
mean, all the evidence is there, I haven't
even attempted to deny it.' Sudden panic
was making her shiver, the prospect of even
now being forced to accept the deadly gift of
freedom.

'Like me, Olga, the police may find it
difficult to believe you capable of killing.'

'But I've explained to them, and to you,
Henry, how it happened. I didn't mean to
kill. I only meant to defend myself – the

instinct of self-preservation – and I just went too far. I mean, surely it's as difficult to believe that Hugo did what he did–'

'Hugo. Ah yes… Darling, I'm only saying that the shock of whatever happened may have distorted your memory. You've been imagining things lately about yourself, you've–'

'I killed Hugo, Henry. I think you must accept that I know whether or not I killed someone.' Absurdly, she now felt annoyed. *Annoyed!* And, somewhere behind the annoyance, surprised that Henry was showing so little reaction to her revelation of Hugo's demented behaviour.

'Oh, Olga, oh my poor darling.' But of course, all his reaction was for his wife.

'They took my fingerprints, Henry, and they asked me a lot of questions before they asked me for my statement.'

'They were bound to do that, Olga.'

She gathered what forces she had left, to try and convince him.

'I didn't imagine not feeling well, Henry, and I didn't imagine killing Hugo.' Desperately she fought to hold his eyes in her glare, and saw a change in them.

'All right, darling,' said Henry thoughtfully, staring at her now in his turn, so searchingly she had to look away. 'I'm so very sorry.' Again, it crossed her mind to be surprised that he was saying nothing about what Hugo had done. 'Yes. If they charge you you'll be remanded in custody.'

'They will charge me.' But her relief at the prospect, even as it suffused her, was swept away on thoughts of the children.

'Martin and Lucy!' Olga tore at her sleeve to get to her watch. 'They'll be home any time after four and I shan't be–'

'They told me in the car this morning that Sadie Porteous was bringing them home. I rang her from the office as soon as I'd heard from the police. Sadie's going to keep them for tea, and I'll collect them when I leave you.'

'Oh, Henry, of course. I should have known you would arrange it.' She was less worried about the children than she had been since the nightmare began, but for the first time she must show concern. And she would be a fool to believe that the threat would entirely disappear. 'Henry... When it gets into the Press... Someone might try to do something – not nice – to the children of a killer.'

'*Don't*... Don't worry, darling, I'll get their days sewn up. And I'll be there in the evenings and at night. Pam will rally. And no doubt a few school mothers. The children will be all right.' He was still looking at her in that disconcerting thoughtful way.

'Thank you, Henry.' There was no point in saying any more, no point in worrying any further. By removing herself from the children she had done all she could for them.

'Olga...' Henry had begun very slightly to fidget, reminding her of those mornings at the front door when they were waiting for Martin. The memory was a knife in her side, and had to be pushed away. 'If – when – they charge you, they'll search you, darling, and take your bag away.'

She turned her hysterical laugh into a cough. But Henry, so solemn in his reluctant revelation, did not know that they – *they* – had taken her bag away the day before, that to have it taken away by the British police was a comparative privilege.

'And, darling... You talked about manslaughter, and of course that's the sort of verdict your counsel would try to secure. But in the first place–'

The door opened, and the WPC shifted her attention.

'Mrs Trent.'

'Yes.' The gravity of the detective-inspector's expression, as he stood just inside the door with a sheaf of papers in his hand, had her on her feet.

'Will you come with me, please.'

This is it, thought Olga, *this is my temporary order of release.* The detective-inspector's heavy demeanour filled the room as pervasively as the big brother voice had filled the cellar where she had perfected her aim.

Henry rose as well.

'I'd better go now,' he said. He wasn't asking a question, he too was making a statement.

'If you will, sir,' said the inspector, briefly informal as he turned away from Olga. 'In the circumstances–'

In the circumstances. They had said that when they had suggested it would be more practical to aim for the head than the heart. Now she couldn't aim at either. Had a potential prisoner ever more willingly entered a cage?

'I understand.' Henry put his arms round her. They would not be round her that night. It must be terrible to go to prison not wanting to. 'Goodbye for the time being, darling. Everything will be all right. I love you and I'll see you soon.'

'I love you too, Henry.' She knew that she did, even though she couldn't feel it. But she couldn't feel anything except hope, with relief just discernible beyond it.

'If you're ready, Mrs Trent.'

'Yes, I'm ready.' It was extraordinary, the way her life had narrowed to a choice between two sets of jailers. 'Goodbye, Henry.'

On her last glimpse of him, his head was bowed. The CID inspector escorted her across the busy lobby, opened the first door in a long dark passage which led off it. The room behind the door was very small, not much larger than the desk behind which stood a man in uniform.

'This is the station sergeant,' the inspector informed Olga as he handed over the papers he was carrying. The station sergeant began immediately to read the top sheet, and after a silent moment looked up at Olga.

'Are you Olga Lubimova Trent of 4 The Crescent, Hopeside Gardens, Kew?' The station sergeant's voice was much deeper and richer than the inspector's.

'I am, yes.' The skin under her left eye was twitching, and she put up her hand to it.

'Please listen carefully to what the inspector will say to you.'

The station sergeant handed the papers back to the inspector.

'You are not obliged to say anything,' said the inspector as he took them, 'unless you wish to do so, but whatever you say will be taken down in writing and may be given in evidence.' His voice lost expression as he began to read. 'Olga Lubimova Trent,' read the detective-inspector slowly and monotonously, 'I charge you that you on the twenty-ninth day of September nineteen-hundred-and-eighty-seven, at Kew in the London borough of Richmond upon Thames, did attempt to murder Charles Hugo Stratton contrary to Common Law.' The inspector looked up from the papers, his voice reverting to its normal tone. 'Do you wish to say anything?'

'Murder... Not murder, manslaughter,' said Olga. She had to lean against the counter. 'It was ... self-defence... I explained...'

'You are innocent of all charges unless and until proved guilty,' said the inspector, briskly but not unkindly. 'That you acted in self-defence will be for your counsel to establish. Do you wish to say anything?'

'No.' That was what Henry had been going to tell her when the inspector came for her. Murder would be the charge, manslaughter the hoped-for mitigation.

The inspector handed the papers back to the station sergeant, who wrote something on them Olga's clouded eyes couldn't or wouldn't read even when the sergeant turned the papers round to face her.

'Just sign your name, please. Here.'

The station sergeant and the detective-inspector also put their signatures to the murder charge before the inspector led her further along the passage.

'Good morning, Mr Trent, let me take your coat. There – we – are! I was very sorry, sir, to read ... to hear...' It had been on the news as well as in the papers.

'Thank you, George. Good of you.'

'We're all sorry, sir.' Really, thought George, as he stood holding Henry's coat and trying to avoid his eye while wishing this particular club member would move on out of the lobby and ease his embarrassment, Mr Trent didn't look all that bad despite the shocking publicity, despite the terrible thing it appeared that his wife had done. In fact, although he was even thinner and paler than George was used to seeing him, he looked almost cheerful, and he certainly wasn't keeping his eyes down or walking like a man with a load on his shoulders. Less stooped than usual, George decided from his oblique glances at Henry, and felt almost shocked. Surely a man should be visibly crushed by such an ordeal? All the same, he liked Mr Trent, had always liked him, one of the best, he hoped the committee wouldn't feel they had to ask him to resign...

'Anyone here this morning, George?'

Mr Trent at last seemed to be on his way. But he was always a cool one. Perhaps, inside, he had had to brace himself.

'There's Colonel Gerrard, sir, and Dr Oversby. Mr Bartholomew—'

'Ah! Thank you, George.'

Henry crossed the lobby, straightening his tie, and entered the reading-room. The first two men George had mentioned, and a couple of others, were spread about in arm-chairs behind newspapers and journals. Each of them, as Henry passed with a murmured greeting, glanced aside as he saw who it was, amended his reflex with a muttered few words, coloured slightly, and looked down again at his reading matter. Embarrassment rather than hostility, Henry knew, inarticulate sympathy probably as well, but he wished they could manage to be normal, they made him feel as isolated as if they had sent him to Coventry.

He found Ian Bartholomew in a chair close to the window, *Punch* open on his lap but staring down on to the busy street below.

'Ian. Are you lunching?'

'Yes. Lunch with me, won't you?' The sharp bright eyes softened as Henry's met them. 'I'm so very sorry.'

'Thanks.' How easy it would be for all his acquaintances, as well as for him, if they simply said the few words Ian had just said. 'And yes, I'd like to lunch with you. As a matter of fact I was hoping–'

'Ah. Henry. Don't take it amiss, but might I – er – offer my condolences?'

'My wife hasn't died, Charles.' Henry smiled at the large man who had followed him across the room, to ease the impact of the sarcasm he hadn't been able to resist. In contrast to Ian Bartholomew and his undefined senior status in the Civil Service, Charles Oversby was an openly eminent psychologist much in demand for royal commissions and television panels, but this was not the first time Henry had reflected that it would be to Charles's social advantage to apply his techniques to his own personal approach. 'Thanks, though.'

'Have lunch,' suggested Charles, unchastened. 'Take your mind off things.'

'I'm just about to. With Ian.' Charles was standing in the wrong place to see the look of resignation pass between the other two men. 'We'll make it a threesome.'

'I'm all right,' said Henry, when they were seated in the remotest corner of the dining-room, where the head waiter had led them without consultation following their departure from the reading-room to a background of slightly more expansive murmurs when it was seen that Henry had managed to collect Ian Bartholomew and Charles Oversby. 'Really I am.' He found himself absurdly anxious that they shouldn't feel embarrassed by him. 'Not that I shall attempt to deny the wretchedness of having to tell the children something, having to fend off the Press, having to–'

'Having to take it in that one's wife–' Charles began to supply.

'Wondering every moment of the day and night how she's bearing up,' corrected Henry. 'Not about why she did it, because she didn't. The police haven't found Hugo's murderer yet, Charles.'

'A bottle of Mouton Cadet?' suggested Ian into the pause. His keen eyes scarcely left Henry's face.

'Fine,' said Henry and Charles, and

Charles went on. 'Your wife confessed, Henry, if the very sketchy Press reports are to be believed.' His eyes, too, were on Henry's face. Professionally.

'Olga did confess, yes, I'm not trying to contradict the facts.' A mutual acquaintance who had not been in the reading-room nodded at their table as he entered the dining-room, but didn't come over. Plates of the day's joint with vegetables were set down in front of them. 'She didn't kill Hugo, though.'

'How do you know?' It was, of course, Charles again. 'I'm sorry, Henry, but those facts you've just mentioned, they're not in favour of your thesis.'

'I know my wife. Olga couldn't kill anyone. She even shoos bluebottles out of the back door.'

'She might shoo one a little more vigorously than she intended, and put paid to it.' Charles might have been on TV, arguing some hypothetical case.

'Don't you think,' ventured Ian, 'that we might change the subject?'

'It's all right,' said Henry. 'I can't think about anything else, anyway.' Glancing across the room, he caught the eye of an attentive member, who looked quickly away.

'Why d'you think your wife said she killed Hugo Stratton then, Henry, if she didn't?' Charles was inclined to talk with his mouth full.

'Olga's suffering from some temporary mental disorder. I'm afraid when she tried to tell me about it I didn't pay much attention. Which was unintelligent of me as well as unkind, knowing as I do that Olga is a stoic and never complains about her health, or her luck, or her lot in life. Something to do, perhaps, with being born and bred in Soviet Russia, but it's her nature, too. Anyway, she'd been trying to tell me for some time that thing weren't right with her, and I just didn't listen.'

'So shooting Hugo Stratton was a cry for help? A somewhat drastic equivalent of stealing from Marks and Spencer's?'

'Confessing to shooting him was.'

'Hm. You don't believe then, Henry, that Hugo Stratton offered your wife any – provocation?'

'He couldn't have done.' *For two reasons.* But he would, of course, mention only one. 'As she didn't kill him, he must have been dead when she arrived at his flat.'

'I see.' Charles was unlikely to be accepting what he was saying, but nothing showed in the concentrated attention of his face. Ian was studying the label on the wine bottle. 'So when your wife found a murder she decided to confess to it to draw attention to her plight.'

'Something like that.' Henry realized in surprise that he had eaten nearly all his roast beef, and most of the Yorkshire pudding. He took a long swallow of wine. 'It happens, Charles. You must have come across it in your work. Women who in their entire right mind are the sanest of the sane, suddenly going haywire.'

'Yes. Oh yes.' The beam of Charles's gaze was mercifully wavering.

'Just cheese, I think?' suggested Ian, beginning a long anecdote which took them through the rest of the meal. As soon as his cheese was finished Charles Oversby pushed back his chair.

'Sorry, must go,' he said. 'And Henry...' Charles blinked, at last looking diffident. 'Forgive me for rather going on, it wasn't the thing. I do tend to get carried away–'

'That's all right, Charles.' Henry's eyes were locked with Ian's.

'Admire your loyalty,' concluded Charles gruffly. 'Hope there's better news...' He got up and charged out of the dining-room.

'Charles's lack of sophistication never ceases to amaze me,' said Ian. 'You wanted to see me, Henry.'

'Yes.' He hadn't realized he had been signalling. Or perhaps it was just that Ian had learned to read body language. 'I did rather want a private word. Have you time for a game of squash?'

'Not the best of occupations immediately after lunch, but yes, I've time for a game.

Let's repair below.'

Neither man was in his first youth, and the play was punctuated by frequent panting against the wall.

'I know you can do it,' gasped Henry, as Ian at last clinched his lead in their one and only game. 'So – will you? No doubt the police will have found the usual diary, and I can supply the names of a few people who knew Hugo Stratton. Female names could be the significant ones, he ran them in tandem. And there was a young man...' He had a sudden vivid inward vision of those moments in Hugo's hall, the last time he and Olga had gone for dinner, as if they were part of a play he had seen – the restless young woman centre stage, the silent immobile one in the background, the second face at the front door, white and angry... 'Will you do it, Ian?'

'Oh yes, Henry,' said Ian Bartholomew, 'I'll do it.'

CHAPTER 8

Even though it was three days since she'd opened the paper and seen the illustrated report, Samantha de Vere still had to keep taking the cutting out of her handbag and re-reading it. She had it on the counter, now, as she shaped up her one and only less than perfect fingernail.

DEATH AT NOON – I KILLED HIM, SAYS RUSSIAN EMIGREE. Thirty-seven-year-old Mrs Olga Trent, her dramatic fine-boned looks the testimony to her early life as a citizen of the USSR, shot Mr Charles 'Hugo' Stratton the well-known London photographer with his own gun before telephoning the police and sitting down to await their arrival...

She knew it, word for word, by heart, yet each time she read it she seemed to be learning something new. *I killed him, says Russian émigrée.* She'd thought there was something – different – about that foreign woman the moment she'd set eyes on her in Hugo's flat. (Hugo was *dead.*) Something odd, not like other people. The funny posh way she spoke, for a start. Not even like an ordinary foreign accent. She just couldn't understand how Hugo could find her so marvellous, asking her advice and so on all the time, talking about her until she, Samantha, had been fed up with her even before they met.

Telephoning the police and sitting down to await their arrival. Just the sort of weird thing the woman would do, she must be crazy...

Hugo was *dead*. She'd seen it first on the television, one of the headline items. A close-up photograph of Hugo smiling, against a background of the news reader saying that he'd been shot dead at his flat and that a woman was helping the police with their inquiries. When she'd got over the shock of it – she still couldn't quite remember what she'd done for a few minutes, but she'd found herself curled up very tight in a chair with her head on her knees – she'd felt sure that the woman must be that weird Mrs Trent. What Englishwoman would telephone the police to tell them she'd murdered someone (whether she had or not), and then sit there waiting for them to come and take her away? Later that same evening they'd said in another TV news bulletin that the woman had been charged. She wouldn't go to prison, she'd go to hospital, they'd know she was ill...

'When you're ready, Samantha.'

'I'm ready, Frank,' said Samantha

graciously, laying down the nail file on the counter and unhurriedly moving the register the few inches necessary to cover it. The Press cutting was already back in her bag, she never risked Frank Cannon taking her unawares when she was reading it, Frank knew nothing about Hugo. Since she'd been – generous – to Frank, he'd been generous to her, never hustling her or telling her off, even by his tone of voice, if she wasn't exactly at the ready when he wanted to give her a letter, or when there was a client waiting. It had been a measure of what she had begun to feel for Hugo, that she'd been seriously considering ceasing her generosity to Frank even though she knew how it would affect her job, could even force her to look for another one. But with her looks and her manner, she wouldn't have any difficulty... Hugo was dead, there was no need to rock the boat at the Miramar Hotel.

Samantha was aware of an unfamiliar prickling sensation at the back of her eyes, but she knew her face, as she turned it towards Frank, would be its usual calm blank.

'A Mr Hargreaves will be arriving at lunch-time, Samantha,' said Frank in a fussy, self-important voice. 'A rather special client for reasons I won't go into. I shall be very much obliged, dear, if you will give him a very special welcome.'

'But of course, Frank.'

Twenty years earlier he mightn't have been bad-looking, reflected Samantha, as she permitted herself a hint of a smile in the direction of her employer. Before the lower part of his face had enlarged so, and those tufts started to sprout out of his ears and nose. It was only by shutting her eyes at a certain moment that she was able to... *A very special welcome.* She'd done that a couple of times before, warily, and been relieved to find that Frank hadn't intended the expression to mean more than it actually said. But then, of course, Frank was the jealous type. If it ever did get to the point where his business instincts took over from his rather pathetic need for care and attention, if she ever was expected to be more than receptionist-cum-secretary, then she really did think she would move on... Hugo was *dead*, did it really matter what she did?

Detective Chief Superintendent Malcolm Harvey of Scotland Yard pushed the set of papers away from him when his coffee was brought in, but was unable to sustain his relief at the distraction. Within seconds of his first sip he had drawn them towards him again and was reading the top sheet through for the third time.

And finding it no less bewildering.

In this instance, though, his not to reason why.

The Chief Superintendent fingered a button on his desk. 'Ask Detective Chief Inspector Hewitt to come and see me, will you, please? With Detective-Sergeant Hughes.'

When the two men arrived he was reading the top sheet for the fourth time.

'Ah, Hewitt. Hughes. Please sit down.'

'Good morning, sir.' Detective Chief Inspector Peter Hewitt was good on atmosphere, and could feel one now. His sergeant's round pink face was turned to him in silent inquiry, and as they both sat down Peter gave him a significant look. 'Something special?'

The Chief Superintendent had to smile, although he didn't feel like it. 'Is it so obvious, Chief Inspector?'

'I don't know, sir, I only wondered...' Peter Hewitt spoke with ostensible self-deprecation. In his head he was singing *Early one morning*.

'The Kew murder,' said the Chief Superintendent, annoying himself that he had said the words as if they were a banner headline.

'The Kew murder, sir? That's pretty well sewn-up, isn't it?'

'It appears, Peter, that it isn't.'

'But, sir... This Mrs Trent, she's confessed, hasn't she? I mean, she rang us, waited for us...'

'There is, I believe, a personality disorder. Not your concern. Or mine. Our concern is

134

to get under way with a murder hunt.'

The Chief Inspector and the Sergeant looked at one another in amazement, then back at their superior officer.

'Mrs Trent has been released, then, sir?' Surprise and shock made Detective-Sergeant Hughes forget that he found it more politic, in the Chief Superintendent's presence, to allow his chief inspector to be his spokesman unless specifically addressed. 'There hasn't been anything in the media—'

'Nor will be for the moment, Sergeant.' Malcolm Harvey paused, trying to find the best words. It might be easier if he himself had some vague idea about what was going on. 'So far as the media is concerned, so far as the public is concerned, Mrs Olga Trent confessed to the murder, was charged, and is in prison awaiting trial. So far as the truth is concerned as well, because that continues to be the situation. Which should have brought your two sets of quick wits to realize that this murder hunt will not be precisely like the usual outfit. It will be unofficial.'

'I don't understand, I'm sorry, sir,' said Detective Chief Inspector Peter Hewitt into the silence.

'I sympathize with you, Peter.' But the Chief Superintendent, despite temptation, would not go quite so far as to say that he was in the same position. 'It's tricky. You'll have to take my word for it that there are –

aspects of the matter – which I'm not in a position to reveal to you.' A paraphrase, if not an exact quotation, of the words which had accompanied that set of papers on to his desk.

'Well – yes, sir,' said Peter Hewitt helplessly. 'But if we're to carry out a murder investigation we'll have to–'

'Ostensibly you'll be investigating the precise movements of Mrs Trent round about the time she killed Charles Hugo Stratton. You'll be buttering people up, Peter, telling them their evidence could be invaluable, making them bask in the revelation of their usefulness to the community, lulling them into what this time really will be a false sense of security. The thing to remember will be regularly to punctuate your inquiries with the reassurance that Mrs Trent has been charged with the crime, and that you're just attempting to sew up the details. It's a tough one, Peter, Geoff, I can't deny it.' Any more than he could deny his own sense of disturbance. Of ruffled pride, even, which was another thing that annoyed him.

'Any particular suspects?' asked the Detective Chief Inspector.

'Ah yes.' This was easier ground. 'Three. Two connected with each other, the third loosely connected with the two. Two young women, and the boyfriend of one. Apparently Stratton was running the women

136

together. One of them was a dinner guest a week or so before the murder, when Mrs Trent and her husband were present, too. We have it on impeccable authority that the second young woman called uninvited at Stratton's flat during the dinner party because of not having heard from Stratton for what she considered to be too long a time, and that she was closely followed by the irate boyfriend.'

The detective-sergeant gave a low whistle, then, his pink facing turning briefly crimson, muttered an apology at which the Chief Superintendent indulgently smiled. 'I know, I know.' And the two men in front of him, they must know, by now, how little control their superior had over this particular turn of events.

'And what transpired, sir?' asked Peter Hewitt politely.

'Stratton appeared to sort things out in a matter of minutes. Apparently–' the Chief Superintendent made a mental note not to use the words *apparently* and *appeared* again – 'the young woman who hadn't been invited was also trying to retrieve the situation and she and her boyfriend left almost at once after she had said her interest in contacting Stratton was professional. She'd been his photographic model already.'

'The other girl?'

'The other girl's a receptionist at a hotel in

137

the Cromwell Road. Dumb blonde. No visible reaction to the incursion.'

'It doesn't absolutely hit one as a scenario for murder,' murmured Peter Hewitt.

'Of course it doesn't,' said the Chief Superintendent testily, completing his hat-trick of annoyance at ultimately failing to keep his sense of disequilibrium to himself. And his second cup of coffee had gone cold. 'But it's the one vouched-for recent episode of conflict in the murdered man's life apart from his confrontation with Mrs Trent, and as such, given this unofficial clean slate, it has to be the place to start the investigation. Now, Peter–' the Chief Superintendent leaned back in his chair, his eye falling less hopelessly on the top file of his In-tray as he saw the conference approaching its end – 'ostensibly working within the current situation is of the essence. Mrs Olga Trent confessed to killing Charles Hugo Stratton, circumstantial evidence bears out her con-fession – I don't have to go into *that* again, thank heaven – and that's exactly how things are so far as everyone is concerned apart from you and me and a few other rather more rarefied souls. And the other people you'll need to help you. Make it as few as possible, and put the fear of God into them as I'm putting it into you.' The Chief Superintendent smiled wanly at his little joke. 'All three suspects could be got out of the way quite easily, of course. Being handed Mrs Trent on a plate right away we haven't had to find out whether they have alibis, and it won't be all that difficult to inquire if they were in a position to have seen Mrs Trent arriving or departing. If they say they weren't, and you can prove it, then that's the end of them.' That's when it would begin to get even worse. 'All right?'

'We can see what's wanted, yes.' Peter Hewitt turned to his detective-sergeant, who belatedly and vigorously nodded. 'But as you said, sir, it's tricky.' Peter paused, realizing something. 'All the same, I rather feel we ought to thank you for the confidence you're placing in us.' He grinned at his superior officer as a surge of that confidence suddenly made itself felt. 'Let's just hope the triangle turns out to be the right figure for the job. Or–' he paused again – 'that someone has third thoughts and says as you were. What happens, I wonder, sir, if we don't find an alternative murderer?'

'That again, Peter, will not be your affair.' It might, though, still just be his, and the Chief Superintendent's incipient sense of relief retreated. He almost wished they'd been passed over in favour of Special Branch – by the look of things, they could have been. He removed the top sheet of the papers still in his hand before indicating the rest. 'It's all here, I'll have it copied and sent through to you before the end of the morning. Then you can get going. You can use the time meanwhile in deciding and recruiting your team. Keep it small, as I said. And secret. And remember that as well as asking these three suspects to help you sew up the case against Mrs Trent, you and your team will have to get the objective angle on their movements the day of the murder from their neighbours, their employers, their local shopkeepers et al. Their families, too, if they have them – I haven't read every word of the dossier–' he had scarcely read beyond that first page– 'but I suspect this particular trio is likely to be rootless. And, of course, there must be absolutely priority for the investigation so far as each and every one of you is concerned.'

'That's understood, sir.' Peter Hewitt got to his feet, his detective-sergeant immediately following suit.

'Report to me with monotonous regularity, Peter,' said the Chief Superintendent, when they were at the door.

'For heaven's sake, Governor!'

Detective-Sergeant Geoffrey Hughes shed his inhibitions before the Chief Inspector's office door was closed on them.

'I meant what I said, Geoff.' Peter Hewitt slumped into his chair. 'The old man must think quite well of us.'

'A government dimension, would you say,

Governor?' asked the Sergeant warily.

'Your guess is as good as mine. Even the old man's guessing, and not much liking the unfamiliar sensation. I'll get Bob Ryan in on it. And Detective-Sergeant Boyle? Or ditto Greene?'

'Boyle, I should say, Governor.' Geoff Hughes sat upright in the other chair where he had flopped down, and Peter Hewitt allowed himself the preliminary self-congratulation – there might not be any more to come – of having at one stroke got the best back-up sergeant for the job and improved his own sergeant's morale.

'We'll need a woman, too. WPC Mitchell?'

'Without a doubt, Governor.'

'Give me an hour, Geoff, to clear up one or two things that won't go away of their own accord, and to do a bit of judicious delegating. Then get those three in here.'

It was easier for Detective-Inspector Bob Ryan and Detective-Sergeant Johnny Boyle than it had been for Peter and Geoff – they had no need to inhibit immediate expression of their disbelief and reluctance. For WPC Elaine Mitchell as well, Peter would have thought, but all she appeared to be experiencing were interest and enthusiasm. Peter had only just completed his task of limited explanation and recruitment when copies of the papers which had been on the Chief Superintendent's desk were brought in, minus one, to his office.

There were five sets, improving Peter's morale, too, in the realization that the Chief Superintendent must have hoped he would decide to operate with a quintet.

'We'll each of us just read all about it, as a start,' said Peter, his eyes already half way down the first page.

Audrey Elsie Pinnington, known as Samantha de Vere, was twenty-one years old and worked as receptionist/secretary at the Miramar Hotel in the Cromwell Road. She lived in a rented bedsitter nearby – so it didn't look as though Charles Hugo Stratton had offered her any patronage – and had a mother and father in a north London suburb who ran a newsagent's. The dossier gave the name of the school she had attended, and the fact that she had gained an O-level in Maths. There was a sister working in another small London hotel (but he was only assuming the Miramar was a modest establishment because he had never heard of it). Miss de Vere had taken a secretarial course on leaving school and had worked thereafter exclusively in hotel reception…

The Chief Superintendent hadn't put it into so many words, but in the peculiar circumstances the questioning of the suspects' families and friends and shopkeepers and so on would have to be an undercover job. As such, the normal necessity for two members of the Force to operate together wouldn't apply, it would be a matter of a nice-mannered, unremarkable young man or woman asking in pub or shop, or even at a front door, if he or she might possibly be put in touch with one or other of the suspect trio. 'I lost touch with Samantha (say) a year or two ago, and regret it. If you don't feel you want to help me make contact with her again, I'd be awfully grateful just to hear how she is...' And before they got on to that, a casual encounter with each suspect could be more rewarding than the approach as policemen... He'd like to do that part of the job himself, but of course he couldn't have it all ways. If he went to Samantha de Vere as a policeman, another member of his team would have to meet her by chance in a café or pub. And vice versa...

Annabel Jane Gordon, read Peter Hewitt from the second sheet, aged twenty-three. Photographic model, living in studio flat in Chelsea. Only child, father and mother extant, father a stockbroker in the City. (So no patronage there either, so far as Charles Hugo Stratton was concerned, and no necessity by the look of it.) Went to private school, six O-levels. (She and Miss de Vere between them catering for the various aspects of Stratton's predilections?) Worked several times for Stratton, and for a number of other London photographers, particularly in advertising. Had long-term on-off relationship with Roger Michael Innes, see below. (Why couldn't the ferrets who had got this far have gone the whole hog?)

Innes was twenty-five and worked in independent television as a floor manager. His parents were dead and had been publicans, and he lived in a bedsitter in Earls Court. He'd left his comprehensive with four O-levels, then gone on to a south London technical college and added a couple of As in Maths and Chemistry. It was thought by both the college and his current employers that he had a promising future. (Well, perhaps he had an alibi for the day of Charles Hugo Stratton's death.)

'All right?' asked Detective Chief Inspector Hewitt, looking round the silent room.

'Why me, Governor?' asked Detective-Sergeant Johnny Boyle.

'Why not you?' Peter countered. 'Seeing that I feel a rather special confidence in you. If, though, Johnny, you yourself really do believe the subtleties of this particular assignment to be outside your range I've no wish to go against–'

'I'll come in with you, Governor, of course I will.' Boyle rubbed the top of his head with the palm of his hand, grinning apologetically.

'Of course!' echoed Detective-Inspector Ryan and WPC Mitchell.

'Good. We're a team. And something tells

me that we'll be doing a job which but for the grace of God could well have been given to Special Branch.' Peter Hewitt beamed round on his still predominantly wary audience, with a smile whose purpose was as much to embolden himself as to encourage the others. 'Unless anyone has a better idea, I suggest we begin by approaching each member of the trio personally and directly, in the statutory pairs. Then, if this fails to eliminate one, two, or three of them through provable alibi, we can go on to the even less official stage of our investigation. That, of course, won't be as police personnel, and it won't necessarily be in twos. Obviously those of us who approach one member of the trio officially will have to lay off anything else so far as that particular individual is concerned – to be recognized would be collective and personal disaster and I doubt if our careers would survive it. I don't have any strong feelings about this, but I suggest Geoff and I approach one of the girls – say Miss Pinnington/de Vere – and Bob and Johnny the other. Then whichever pair finishes first can go on to the boy. After that, with the one or ones who are still in contention, we can engineer casual meetings and go through their homes and their belongings before making contact with their nearest if not necessarily dearest – Miss de Vere's hotel manager, for example, landlords and landladies, local shops, friends when we've discovered who they are. This is where Elaine will come into her own. In fact, so far as the two girls are concerned if not the boy, Elaine is probably more likely than the rest of us to make innocent-seeming contacts and not excite comment on landings.'

'Goody!' exclaimed WPC Mitchell, hunching her shoulders as she pressed her hands down between her knees. Peter Hewitt's confidence that she was by no means as naïve as she looked remained unshaken.

'Refer to the Chief Superintendent anyone who tries to tell you that what you're doing is not your first priority,' said Peter, thinking of the muscle-flexing CI with whom Bob Ryan currently tended to be working. 'It is in fact your absolute priority, as he will explain to anyone who attempts to complain to him about your lack of cooperation. We'll meet again tomorrow late afternoon, to pool the information and impressions we've gathered.' He was aware of a couple of sharp movements. 'Yes, I know it isn't very long, but we're not going to hang about and it'll give us time enough to get the overt contacts over, and the covert ones under way.'

CHAPTER 9

Annabel Gordon rolled over on to her back and stretched her arms out above the bedclothes, aware of nothing but the dawning physical sensations of comfort and health. As the cool air turned cold on her skin she drew her arms lazily back under cover, let her hands trace the approved concave of her stomach between the two sharp pelvic bones. Her eyes were scarcely open but she was aware of light through the thin curtains, she ought to be turning her head to look at the clock by her bed...

Hugo is dead.

The memory which the innocence of sleep had destroyed flooded back through her like a stream of poison, so that she drew her thin body into a circle on an instinct to shorten the long shafts of pain.

Don't love me, Annabel, please don't love me. Just like me a lot.

The last dreadful words Hugo had said to her she couldn't yet manage to think about, but this other, earlier, desolation she couldn't get out of her head. She'd pretended at the time that she would do as he wished, but instead of heeding his warning

147

she had gathered the cold, pleading words to her heart as the foundation, after all, of the love he was denying her. Telling herself that now he had confessed to his fear of love he would be 'more relaxed', and she and love would be able to creep up on him unawares...

'Fool!' shouted Annabel Gordon, pressing her knees up under her chin. Even when he'd made love to her he hadn't really been there, as he'd been there when they'd talked and laughed and gone hand-in-hand to look at strange and beautiful things in and out of London. Why hadn't she settled for that hand-in-hand, for bear hugs, for affectionate friendship? That was what she and Hugo had naturally grown into, but she had been greedy, she hadn't found it enough, although now she would give everything she had in the world to get it back again.

But Hugo was dead...

Even in the early days, when she'd worked regularly with him and they'd started seeing each other outside the studio following a late photographic session and a sudden mutual desire for Chinese food – oh, if only she had cherished those beginnings! – she'd been aware that she didn't fit into the pattern of his life.

'Fool!' she called out again, remembering that at the time she had seen this as her strength rather than her weakness. She had actually been encouraged by the fact that she was different from Hugo's usual girlfriends, his statuesque blondes, brunettes, and redheads without brains or conversation. The most beautiful had undoubtedly been the magnificent creature whose image standing by right in Hugo's hall when she had so madly gatecrashed his dinner party was still clear in her mind's eye. It was after that that Hugo had suggested, oh so gently, that it would probably be better if they went their ways.

'You know how it is with me, Annie dearest,' he'd said apologetically. 'I just can't live with anything serious. It's a fearful defect in my character, I'm all too aware of it, but I'm afraid it's me.'

'But, Hugo, I don't have to be serious, I wasn't serious, we weren't either of us serious in the beginning, I mean, we...' She had gabbled at him, begging him with a lack of sophistication the memory of which even now made her jerk with embarrassment. 'Hugo, let's be as we were, we had so much fun together, Hugo, you know we did, you—'

'Look, love.' He had put his hands on her shoulders, she had thought: *He is touching me for the last time,* and the moment was so terrible she could scarcely sustain it. 'One can't go back, you know. It isn't possible. We did have fun, yes, I'm grateful for it. I'll remember it. But when two people cease to see a relationship in the same way...'

She had to stop her exact memories at that point. Groaning, Annabel shifted on to her other side and squinted at her clock. Just past eight, and she had a photographic session at nine. Thank God for work.

She didn't have all that much time, but she didn't get up right away because despite switching off her precise recollections she was still left with the puzzle of that Russian woman who had confessed to the murder of Hugo. She had only seen her for a few moments during that terrible time inside Hugo's front door – her mind swung dizzily – but she had seemed so sane, so calm, it had been that woman's large dark eyes which had brought her, Annabel, to her senses and made her try to salvage what she could from her crazy stupidity. And Hugo had mentioned her quite often, he valued her opinion and her friendship and the mental stimulus of conversation with her, though in a way which had never given Annabel the slightest pang of jealousy. But if Olga Trent had telephoned the police to tell them she had killed Hugo with his own gun, there must have been something more between them. When it came to the trial, of course, and maybe even before, she would see and hear in the media what Mrs Trent had to say, which might throw some light...

What did it matter now, Hugo was *dead*.

As she rolled wearily out of bed, her body no longer telling her it was young and strong, Annabel was aware for the first time of a sensation which brought with it a very slight reduction of her misery. For a few moments, standing naked before her long mirror with her arms raised behind her head, her hands bunching her long dark hair to her skull, she was unable to identify it, or perhaps didn't want to, but as she stared in the gloom at the shadowed oblongs of her eyes and her parted lips, she had to recognize it as relief. Part of her was *glad* Hugo was dead. Glad she no longer had to think of him making love to another woman, putting his hands on another woman's shoulders (to say hello rather than goodbye), taking another woman's hand to lead her somewhere rich and strange. *Oh, Hugo, you and I would still be doing that if I hadn't wanted more than you could give me.* The worst thought, worse even than... The thought she really had to keep away from was the thought that she perhaps *had* had a unique relationship with Hugo, that there might never have been another girl for him to go hand-in-hand with down mean or marvellous streets. Friendship wasn't subject to the ebb and flow of a sexual relationship, and she and Hugo might have gone on together for the rest of their lives...

Hugo's life was over. She wouldn't, after

all, be mourning her destruction of what might have been his one abiding association. He was dead.

And Roger was alive.

Thinking about Roger, mused Annabel as she dressed, was the same remedy for absolute misery as work, bringing with it all the shallow reactions of the everyday – anxiety, irritation, curiosity, weariness. Roger had been beside himself with rage following the brainstorm which had taken her to Hugo's in the middle of a dinner party to which she hadn't been invited. Hugo himself had taken the immediate fire out of the situation, but it had all boiled up in Roger again by the time they got back to his place, and her memory of the rest of the evening was of drooping in a chair beside his old gas fire, hearing his voice rise and fall as he paced about the room, being pulled by him to her feet and shaken like a rag doll before being thrown across his bed and then...

Why did life turn out so sordid and so ugly when it was capable of so much beauty? Suddenly and inescapably Annabel thought of what she had done for Hugo in the making of that terrible photograph, what Hugo's surreal artistic urge had done both to her and to his subsidiary cast when they had assembled to record the evil, left-hand side of his diptych. All at once her lament for her lost innocence, for the eager, open person she had been when she had come to London such a very few years ago, was as acute as the ache in her for Hugo. And yes, there was something in her which was glad he was dead.

Well, she couldn't bring back the self she had been, but she could do one thing – symbolically she dowsed her face in cold water – she could wipe the slate clean.

She would start, obviously, by getting rid of Roger. At least she had retained sufficient sanity to insist on keeping her own flat, so it wouldn't entail any practical adjustments in her life. Nor, now she thought about it, would it be likely to entail the appalling scene which only a week or so ago would have been the inevitable consequence of her telling Roger she had had enough of him. Since the terrible night of that dinner party, Roger had changed. He'd been determined to go round and see Hugo, tell him what he thought of him and all that kind of rubbish, and she had been amazed when he had come back so – so subdued. Fearfully she'd asked him what had happened, and he had just said it was all right, he realized he'd been making a fuss about nothing. That *nothing* had made her hurt and indignant, but she had just put it down to Hugo's cleverness and made herself concentrate on what a relief it would be not to have Roger going on about her and Hugo any more.

But then Roger had changed. Become in fact much more reasonable, much easier to cope with. And for why? Annabel asked herself as she made coffee. Because, she was realist enough to see, he no longer cared so much, it was no longer his primary necessity that Annabel Gordon should be there when he called her. Since Roger had been to see Hugo he'd seemed at times almost as if he was sleepwalking, as if he wasn't really there. It wasn't just that the fire had gone out of his attitude towards her, Annabel, it was as if he was seeing everyone and everything else differently, as well. She'd mentioned the change in Roger to Hugo that last time, before... She'd even made a joke of it, asking Hugo what on earth he'd said to Roger, thanking him for getting Roger off her back. Hugo had just laughed in his mysterious way, saying something about not having found Roger very difficult to deal with, and that he was glad for her that he'd at last started to behave himself. It was only the final part of that last meeting that she remembered verbatim, but she remembered her absurd pain because Hugo wasn't jealous of Roger.

Perhaps it was only that Roger had found another girl who had knocked him overboard – Annabel remembered her own sensations when she had first realized what she felt about Hugo. If this was the sort of thing that had happened to Roger, her decision to be done with him would be far less of a grand gesture than she would have liked. Examining her reactions as she pulled on her coat, Annabel saw that regret at the diminishment of her gesture was all she felt at the prospect of Roger meeting her half way. There was no jealousy, no forlornness. She really would be glad for Roger to go.

But Hugo… How could she have thought she was glad that the world was empty of Hugo?

Don't think about Hugo, Annabel told herself as she started her car, *think about anything and anyone else.* As she made the most of the limited opportunities for movement about the rush-hour streets, she thought again of the tall elegant woman with the large dark eyes who had helped her to retreat from Hugo's dinner party with dignity. Wondered for the umpteenth time why she had said what she had. Hugo would never have attacked her, he would never have attacked anyone. It was almost as if Olga Trent had *wanted* to go to prison… Which would be just as well, seeing that she had been charged with Hugo's murder…

There was a pain under Annabel's ribs, and she felt breathless. Determinedly she switched her thoughts to the assignment for which she ought just to be in time.

She didn't want to think about Olga Trent, either.

'Samantha de Vere?' inquired Peter Hewitt pleasantly, as he and Detective-Sergeant Geoffrey Hughes completed their stroll across the small, busily decorated lobby of the Miramar Hotel in Cromwell Road.

The girl took her time, first over raising her eyes from her fingernails, and then over tucking the nail file under the edge of the hotel register. She was cool. And stunningly beautiful. Peter heard his sergeant catch his breath.

'I'm Miss de Vere. Yes. What can I do for you?'

Poured into their roles, girls like this, reflected Peter. Told to ask *What can I do for you?* and always asking just that, never varying it, never seeing one thing in one customer, something else in another, unless the possibility of sexual attraction entered the equation. And even then, never showing that it did, never venturing, always waiting to see...

'We're police officers, Miss de Vere,' said Geoff, displaying his ID, when he decided the Chief Inspector had left it a few seconds too long. 'We've come to ask you if you can possibly help us.'

It was a pity, thought Peter as he held out his own card, that phrases such as 'helping the police with their inquiries' had developed so sinister a connotation – there were times such as this when it was vital to convey no more than the face value of the words. Varying them of course helped a bit, but not usually as much as was desirable...

'A Mrs Olga Trent has been charged with the murder of Charles Hugo Stratton,' he said swiftly. 'You'll have read or heard in the media, Miss de Vere, how straightforward this particular case appears to be, but even with the simple cases the Crown must seek to discover every discoverable fact before a defendant is brought to court. What we would like–'

A man and a woman came in through the swing door, abruptly destroying the illusion of privacy.

'If you'd like to come through,' said Miss de Vere composedly. With another leisurely gesture she raised the jointed piece of simulated mahogany counter and indicated to the two policemen to follow her behind the curtain beyond it. 'Do sit down,' she said, 'and I'll be with you when I've seen to this lady and gentleman.'

'I was horribly rude to my grandmother once,' said Geoff Hughes *sotto voce,* as they each sat down in a square-cut rust-coloured armchair circa nineteen-thirty-five. 'She said "That gentleman at the bus stop," and I said, "Oh, so you know he's a gentleman, do you, Grandma?" It's either old-fashioned or genteel, isn't it, Governor?'

157

'I would agree with you, Sergeant.' He was assessing the neat sanctum, the one shelf of tidy files, the small desk with covered typewriter, pristine-paged notebook and ballpoint, the 'thirties grate of green and orange tiles fronted by an unlit single bar electric fire. The small room was chilly. Peter could imagine Miss de Vere's bed-sitter to be as uncommunicative. 'A self-possessed young lady?'

'Afraid so. No visible reaction to our identity or our request.'

'None.'

'Sorry to keep you waiting,' said Samantha de Vere as she slowly raised the curtain and reappeared. 'Lucky it was just a straightforward booking.' Peter wondered if this girl would normally have used the word 'straightforward' in connection with room reservations at the Miramar Hotel, or had retained it from their short exchange at the counter. 'Now, you were saying ... Inspector, is it?' As Miss de Vere sank gracefully down on the chair in front of the typewriter the beautiful brown eyes turned without inquiry on to Peter.

'Chief Inspector, actually,' said Peter, as casually as he could. 'And Sergeant Hughes. As I was saying–' he could have done without saying it again– 'Mrs Trent has confessed to the murder of Mr Stratton, and from the fact that she's been charged with the crime it's pretty clear that investigations have borne out her confession. However – and this is entirely routine–' it was, of course – 'the police have to fill in the facts from other points of view as well as the point of view of the defendant, Mrs Trent, so that the Crown will have the fullest information on which to proceed with its prosecution.' There was still no expression in those impassive eyes, and no retreat or even hesitation when they met his. Peter felt he had done rather well, but even if he had been clumsy enough to frighten the girl, he somehow couldn't imagine the fear showing in her face. 'Mr Stratton's address book and diary have revealed the names of his friends, and we know as well, of course, from Mrs Trent herself, that you and she were present at the same dinner party given by Mr Stratton shortly before his death.'

'Yeah, that's right,' responded Miss de Vere. Her eyes, before she dropped them to her full-skirted lap to discover a piece of thread and flick it away, were still blank and uninterested.

'Did you notice anything that you could call unusual that evening, Miss de Vere? Anything, that is, so far as Mr Stratton and Mrs Trent were concerned?' In their ignorance of the reason for their assignment, Peter and his team had decided that to ask a few questions about the dinner party could provide a dual advantage: as well as helping to allay any suspicions Miss de Vere might be harbouring about their real intentions, it might also reveal for their personal inform- ation some unexpected nugget regarding the mysterious Mrs Trent.

'I hadn't met Mrs Trent before, so I don't really see how I could know.'

The response was reasonable. Peter thought there had been a very slight em- phasis on the words *Mrs Trent*.

'No, of course not, we appreciate that, Miss de Vere. Perhaps you could tell us, though: did Mr Stratton and Mrs Trent appear to be on good terms?'

For a few seconds Miss de Vere was silent, examining one of her perfect rosy finger- nails. 'On good terms, yes,' she eventually said, looking up at Peter then slowly turning her eyes to Geoff. 'Very good terms. Although I hadn't met her before, I knew about her. Mr Stratton–' another genteel- ism, thought Peter – 'was always talking about her, he used to ask her opinion, and he often used to say what she thought about things on the news and so on.'

'Thank you, Miss de Vere, that's just the sort of thing we want. Did Mr Stratton ever give you the idea there was anything – of a romantic or sexual nature – in his friendship with Mrs Trent?'

'No,' said Miss de Vere. 'Never.' Her hands were together on her lap now, and the skin was so smooth and golden it was impossible to know whether the knuckles were clenched.

'Thank you. Now, Miss de Vere, to the day of Mr Stratton's death, and I apologize in advance for having to take you over what must be very distressing ground for you.'

'That's all right, if you have to ask everyone.'

'Yes, I'm afraid we do. And what we would most like to discover, of course, is someone who actually saw Mrs Trent arriving at Mr Stratton's flat. So with a mad optimism–' he made himself laugh, and was appalled both by the dismal sound of it and by Miss de Vere's total lack of reaction – 'we're asking everyone this as our first question about that day: were you in a position between say twelve-thirty and one o'clock to see anyone arriving either at Belmont Gardens, or at the front door of Mr Stratton's flat? I'm sorry, Miss de Vere, it's a ridiculous question, but we haven't of course had to question anyone in this case, with Mrs Trent giving herself up, and so there just might be a bit of luck for us somewhere, and why not start at the top? Is there any remote chance that you can help us?'

'I'm sorry,' said Samantha de Vere, staring at him. 'I did have lunch with Mr Stratton sometimes, but not that day.' Wise girl, thought Peter Hewitt, seeing in his mind's eye the neat pages of Charles Hugo Stratton's diary. Some of them said *Sam – lunch*. 'Actually–' Miss de Vere paused, and Peter wondered how much these spaces were a ploy, how much the need for inward effort when circumstances forced the girl to give voice to any kind of a complex thought – 'I don't like to take much of a lunch hour. I'm Mr Cannon's only receptionist, if I go out he has to stay round the counter himself. Of course if I've made an appointment and I ask him–' Samantha looked down again at her lap, smoothed the lavish folds of her skirt – 'he's always pleased for me to go.'

'If you're not well, or have to go to the dentist, say?' asked Geoff Hughes.

'Oh, then Mr Cannon calls on Mrs Whitworth. She's a neighbour of his and will come in for a morning or an afternoon. And when I'm on holiday.'

'A very good arrangement,' approved Peter genially. 'But I can understand why you don't make a habit of long lunch hours. Mr Cannon is very fortunate to have so loyal a receptionist.'

'Secretary/receptionist,' said Samantha de Vere. Peter thought she had preened very slightly, her only visible reaction as yet to anything he and Geoff had said.

'Secretary/receptionist, of course, forgive me. So you were nowhere in the vicinity of Mr Stratton's flat the day he died, Miss de Vere?'

162

'No, I've told you. I did go out that lunch hour, but only for a sandwich and a bit of local shopping.'

'Would you tend to eat your sandwich or whatever in a café, or bring it back here?' asked Geoff humbly.

'Depends how I feel. If it's a rotten day I might bring it back here, sit by the fire.'

'That would be nice and cosy,' said Peter, wishing he and his sergeant were doing it. 'That particular day? It isn't important, of course,' he added swiftly, 'it's just to get things straight so that it's on record you've told us all you can.'

'That day I stayed out. I remember because of seeing on the news that evening…' Even now, her only reaction was to pause again. 'I was busy and I didn't want to take the time when I got back to start eating. So I squeezed on to a stool in the sandwich bar along the road. I expect you'll have to take my word for that, there was such a crowd you could hardly move, nobody'll remember seeing me.'

'Oh, that's all we want, Miss de Vere, we're most grateful to you.' Miss de Vere, surely, was the sort of woman who would expect to be remembered wherever she went, however dense the crowd, and it was out of character for her so to deprecate her impact. And she *would* be remembered, too, looking like she did. But if she went regularly to this sandwich bar, it wouldn't be so easy for its management and its clientele to be precisely sure that Samantha de Vere had made one of her memorable appearances on the day of Stratton's death... Peter's spirits, which had begun to rise, abruptly plummeted.

'You go to this sandwich bar regularly?' he asked, hoping he sounded casual.

'Oh yes,' said Miss de Vere. 'I always get sandwiches there. For Mr Cannon as well. It's only bed and breakfast at the Miramar, the kitchen staff have gone by eleven.'

'I see.' Peter got to his feet, closely followed by his detective-sergeant. 'Thank you again, Miss de Vere, for all your assistance. I hope Mr Stratton's other friends will prove as helpful and cooperative. Mr – Cannon, is it? He's out at the moment?'

'He's holding a business conference in one of the bedrooms,' said Miss de Vere, without irony. 'If you'd like to see him...?'

'Oh no, that won't be necessary.' It wouldn't, at this stage. There was no doubt in Peter's mind that Samantha de Vere had left the hotel for a short lunch hour the day Charles Hugo Stratton had died, and the manager of the Miramar Hotel could add nothing to the fact she had so innocently – so cleverly? – vouchsafed them. 'Good morning, Miss de Vere, and thank you for so willingly sparing us your time.'

'No trouble, I'm sure.'

164

'If there's anything else you remember which you feel might be of help to us–' Peter handed her his card – 'that's my number. Don't hesitate to get in touch.'

'All right. Yes.'

Miss de Vere accompanied them as far as the counter, where she remained. Glancing back in the second before he entered the swing door, Peter saw her minimally move the hotel register and extract her nail file, her face as untroubled and impassive as it had been throughout the interview. ('Little talk', she would most likely call it when relaying the encounter to her employer.)

But: *I did have lunch with Mr Stratton sometimes. That day I stayed out.*

Audrey Elsie Pinnington was still in contention.

CHAPTER 10

'Very shortly now,' said Roger Innes. 'Ready to record. Cue VTR. Ten seconds... Five...'

'Fine, Roger, fine.' The director's voice nestled cosily in his ear. Normally Roger would have congratulated himself on a troublefree take, but today, again, he was scarcely aware of achieving it. He glanced up into the tall blackness above the brilliantly lit section of studio, as always finding that close insinuating voice hard to reconcile with the godlike remoteness of his director on recording days, translated from the hurly-burly of the studio floor aloft to that remote technological oblong of light hanging in space under the distant invisible ceiling, from where his stream of advice and exhortation was conveyed to the earphones around Roger's head.

Not always cosily, of course. If the director wasn't happy... They'd moved now from one set to another, darkness had settled back on the scene they had left and the two temporarily redundant actors who had remained to relax in its gloom, and the lights were shrieking down on another corner.

'Get that reluctant bitch into the right

place, will you, Roger,' ordered the director wearily. 'And you might suggest that Kay gets her nose picked *before* the cameras roll.'

'Great,' said Roger automatically to the actors peopling the set in front of him, frozen into their opening attitudes like a waxwork *tableau vivant.* 'Great. If you could just move that fraction nearer the table, Jennifer darling, you'll remember we decided it would be a better place for you to start from... Hands *away* from your face perhaps, Kay, then you can raise them more dramatically to your head... Great,' he said again, 'that's really good. We'll go now for a rehearsal.'

Spontaneous translation had nothing on this. While he was speaking his director was speaking too, loading the next set of bullets Roger had to fire on his behalf while Roger was still delivering the last lot. It was just as well he was so used to the job he did most of it on a reflex, he was pretty certain no one in the studio had the least idea he'd been pole-axed, that he wasn't really there among them...

'Jack wasn't quick enough on the draw, Roger, for heaven's sake jolly him up a bit. Kay seems to have it right at last but I'm still uneasy about Jennifer.'

'OK, OK,' said Roger to the cast, 'but we'll rehearse again. Quicker, Jack, please, if you can...'

They got that one, too, on the first take.

'Not a bad morning, Roger,' decreed the director. 'Think we'll break there.'

'We'll break there,' Roger told them. 'It's been a good morning. Back here, all of you, please, at two.'

'Coming up for a spot of lunch, Roger?'

He'd tried to slide out before anyone asked him that question, but it was easy enough to tell his chief cameraman that he had a headache.

'Still lots to get through this afternoon, Bill, think I'll try to walk it off. I'll stop by somewhere for a sandwich. See you.'

No point in running the risk of putting himself in the way of comment when there was no need to. Hugo hadn't been found dead after his first visit, and he didn't think anyone knew about the others. Besides, he liked his own company best at the moment, he still hadn't managed to sort out the kaleidoscope of fear, disgust, excitement, surprise, and pain which was the inside of his head.

It was one of those deeply settled autumn days which made him think of a fuzzy-edged Victorian watercolour, a small central intensity of warmth and colour beginning and ending in mist. He bought the sandwich at the first sandwich bar he passed, and sat down to eat it on a seat in the gardens round the corner from the studio, relieved as he looked furtively about him to see that none of his colleagues had had the same idea. He could, of course – he did – continue to push his way through the dazzle of the last weeks even when he was with other people, even when he was with Annabel, but when he was alone he could really, deeply, concentrate on his extraordinary experience.

He'd gone to see Hugo the first time full of fury and indignation. Annabel had denied being more than 'affectionate friends' with him, but you didn't suddenly jump up and rush away from your lover – your lover-to-be that very night, she had known how the land lay – and ring a man's doorbell and then go inside his flat even when you saw he was giving a dinner party to which you hadn't been invited and another dishy girl had. Apart from that night, though, Annabel had been so obviously distracted by Hugo she'd shown it in a thousand ways and been stupid – or indifferent – enough (involuntarily he shuddered) to believe he hadn't noticed.

If Hugo had made her happy it would have been different, thought Roger piously, secure in his knowledge that this could never now come to pass. Then, as he sat there on the bench, pain without warning took over the pattern, great red blobs of bloodstained pain symmetrically predominated that ever-changing kaleidoscope. *Hugo could never make Annabel happy now, and he couldn't make him, Roger, happy either.* Or sad, or shocked, or excited, or fevered out of his mind...

When he had arrived all steam and fury on Hugo's doorstep Hugo had stood aside and said simply, 'Come in and talk about it.' Looking back, Roger thought it was probably then, at that moment, that the enchantment – the black magic? – had begun to work. He had followed Hugo across the hall, and they had stood somewhere in the middle of Hugo's sitting-room staring at one another, and Hugo had become the only person in the world, the only source of pleasure, and pain, and excitement, and frenzy, and fear...

When he got home Annabel had been asleep in his bed, and he had crawled relieved into the tiny slit of a room next door. He'd gone back to see Hugo at the time Hugo had suggested, then back again. Then back again, and the mid-afternoon edition of the *Evening Standard* had carried that banner headline.

It had been so short, so quickly over, so utterly different from anything in his life before, it should be easy for him, now, to let the normal tenor of his life close over it, a stone floor over a flooded cellar. To think of it as a dream. Or a nightmare.

But it could be worse – or less ephemeral – than a nightmare. What if it had permanently changed him? Brought a side of himself to his notice which he hadn't known existed? Since his first visit to Hugo it had been an effort for him to take Annabel in his arms, he had suddenly understood the historic trauma of women struggling to feign ecstasy.

But even before Hugo, his relationship with Annabel had begun to deteriorate. Even before *her* relationship with Hugo – a strange sensation, to be jealous of Annabel rather than jealous of a man on her account – she had been growing restless. (It was a measure of the change in him, the new uncertainty, that he should be admitting to himself that even before Hugo he had not been the total answer to Annabel's prayers.) So perhaps when he had recovered from his weariness, his shock, his pain, and his dizzy memories of his pleasure, he would find himself as he had been before, dutifully assessing the charms and potentialities of every attractive young woman with whom he came into contact.

That wasn't the entire point though, was it?

He didn't know yet whether he would be confining this old and tried routine to the female sex.

Sitting on his bench in the small garden, staring round warily at a world he now only half understood, Roger Innes shivered again, seeing the hands sweeping crumbs from his knees as if they belonged to another man, as if he was no longer to have control of them.

It had been a nightmare. It had been a beautiful dream. But he didn't want it to spill over into his waking life. And perhaps there was hope for him. Whatever it had been, it was irrecoverably over.

Only then did Roger remember the woman at the public centre of events, Mrs Olga Trent, and spend a few moments wondering what part she had really played in the story of Hugo Stratton.

'Is there somewhere we could talk?' asked Detective Inspector Robert Ryan smilingly.

The girl's large eyes swivelled warily from his to Detective-Sergeant Boyle's.

'What about that little park round the corner?' persisted Bob Ryan, struggling to sound even gentler and even less official. 'We're police officers but we're here on very much of an offchance that you might be able to help us and so we're not bringing out our IDs while so many of your workmates are around.'

She wasn't his type, thought Bob Ryan, but she was a thoroughbred and obviously some men would say she was a beauty. He'd sent word that Bob Ryan would like to see Annabel Gordon when she had a break in her session, and he and Johnny Boyle had sat in the lush hot waiting-room for all of forty-five minutes, watching the exotic comings and goings and not minding the delay because just now there was nothing else they ought to be doing.

'Sorry to have kept you waiting so long,' she had said breathlessly, turning her head slightly as she pushed back her long dark hair so that Bob saw the gleam of sweat on her temple and cheek.

Then she had stared at them, frowning, a very slight tic starting to work under an eye. 'I don't think I know either of you.'

Now he had managed to relax her a bit. 'All right,' she said. 'We're breaking for half an hour.'

'We'll go and book a seat,' said Bob, to make her feel better again. And anyway, she ought to refuse to leave a building alone with two strong men who had merely told her they were the law. 'See you round the corner in a few minutes.'

'Thank you.' She had taken his point and she had a radiant smile. When it receded it made him realize how nervy and uneasy she was.

He and Johnny had scarcely sat down in the warm yellow sunshine when she was there, hesitating a moment before fitting warily into the space on the wooden seat awaiting her between them.

The two IDs met just above her lap.

'Yes,' she said. She was holding herself pretty tightly, Bob Ryan thought. Perhaps in

173

an effort to control the trembling which might vibrate through the wooden slats of the seat. 'It must be about Hugo.'

'It is,' he said gratefully. But he had known at once that she was intelligent. He went through the routine they'd more or less worked out before their team conference broke up. He had the impression, all the way, that she was with him or ahead of him. It was a hazard of their curious exercise which he hadn't envisaged, the fear as he spoke that she would see through his explanation as to why he and Johnny had sought her out. 'It's the most absurd long shot,' he ended up, 'but – did you by any chance see Mrs Olga Trent arriving either at Belmont Gardens, or at Charles Hugo Stratton's flat, sometime between half past twelve and one o'clock?'

He glanced at her for long enough to register her uneasy, suspicious look, then stared ahead of him at the plaque on the park wall commemorating the generosity of its founder, uncomfortably aware that she was examining his profile.

'I'm afraid not, Inspector.' She paused. 'I could have done,' she resumed firmly, 'but I didn't. I could have been in Hugo's flat at lunch-time, but I wasn't.' On other days she had been – in his mind's eye Bob Ryan saw the neat diary entries: *Annie – lunch*. 'I remember that day because of … because of switching on the radio when I got home and hearing the news. I had a lunch-time gap between two photographic sessions, and as I wasn't all that far from home after the morning one, I went back to my flat for coffee and a sandwich. Lay on the floor with my legs higher than my head, if you want to know, but without a witness.'

'Goodness!' said Bob heartily, thinking as he spoke that heartiness was not the best manner to adopt towards highly intelligent people, 'it isn't *you* who is to go on trial, Miss Gordon, we're not here to ask you for *your* story.' Did he really need to be so scrupulously dishonest, particularly with someone who was unlikely to be thus slickly reassured?

'I appreciate that, Inspector.'

Bob Ryan turned to look at her again, and saw that her face had relaxed. She had, after all, been prepared to have her anxiety allayed.

'So you can't help us. Well, as I said, it was a long shot. Thank you at any rate, Miss Gordon, for your cooperation.'

'May I ask you a question, Inspector?'

'You may ask.' Bob grinned at her, partly in his relief that his official role in the affair might well be over. It all depended on how quickly Peter and Geoff got through with Miss de Vere.

'How did you know I was a friend of Mr Stratton's?'

175

'Anyone who knows anything about photography knows you worked with him,' said Johnny Boyle, eliciting a little bow and an ironic smile from the apparently restored Annabel Gordon. 'So far as the friendship's concerned – he kept the usual address book and diary.'

'Yes. Of course.'

'So we've got a lot of long shots to fire,' said Bob, taking the opportunity of reinforcing the insignificance of their presence to each side of her.

'I wish you luck.'

Did she?

'I'm sorry I can't help you.'

Couldn't she? And if she couldn't, was she sorry? When she had switched on her radio that evening, had the news of Stratton's death come as a shock to her?

All they had learned from Annabel Gordon was that they had initially alarmed her, and that she was still in contention.

When they got back to the office there was no sign of Detective Chief Inspector Hewitt or Detective-Sergeant Hughes, and no note. Bob and Johnny got themselves a snack, then hung about for half an hour talking desultorily about the lack of progress and not quite meeting each other's eyes. Bob told himself he was reluctant to tackle Roger Innes because he preferred the idea

176

of the undercover role, but he wasn't sure if this was true. At one point he tried to get in touch with WPC Mitchell, but she was out. Eventually Bob wrote '*R.I. – Festival TV Studios – 2p.m. Ryan and Boyle*' on a piece of paper, and as he was trying to put it discreetly but noticeably on Peter Hewitt's desk Peter came into his office.

'All right,' said Peter at once. 'If you and Johnny would like to take on Innes. You were ready first.'

'Whatever you think, Governor.' Bob Ryan tore the piece of paper into little bits and threw them into Peter's wastepaper basket. 'We can't knock Annabel Gordon out. She says she wasn't round Stratton's flat at the significant time, but that she could have been. How about Miss de Vere?'

'She said much the same thing. And no reactions.'

'Oh, Miss Gordon had reactions. Intense nervousness to start with, which she got over as she apparently took us at face value. Frankly, I was afraid she wouldn't, she's pretty bright.'

'Miss de Vere seems pretty thick. Or it may be deep. Whatever, she gave absolutely nothing away. Did you get anything at all from Annabel Gordon about what she thought of Stratton and/or his death?'

'Not really. Well, not at all, except that she looked as if she'd been through the mill.

Although if you don't know what a person looked like before disaster struck, you don't know whether or not they've changed.'

'The classic dilemma in a murder case.' Peter sighed. 'Geoff and I should have been back ages ago. It was the traffic rather than Miss de Vere which detained us. D'you really want to take on Innes, Bob?'

'D'you want two undercovers, Governor?' asked Bob Ryan, grinning.

In the end they tossed a coin, and Peter won. He decided to put himself and Geoff Hughes in as the last official partnership because he felt it was probably the right thing to do.

They had to wait a long time for Innes to emerge from his studio. Peter learned while they sat side by side on the low tweedy seat in the studio foyer, flanked by potted palms, that his sergeant had a cousin who was a TV studio floor manager, and how impossible it was to extricate him from a filming session unless and until his director decreed a break. Geoff Hughes must have offered this reassurance five or six times before a slight dark man with a tense pale face at last came rapidly up to them.

'Yes? I have a message that you want to see me. I only have a few moments.'

'We appreciate that, Mr Innes.' Peter went through what already felt like his familiar routine more warily than he had gone through it with Miss de Vere. Roger Innes was like a frightened colt which could all too easily shy away from them if they didn't get their reassurance in pretty quickly. It was a triumph, he felt, to have Innes within a few minutes actually sitting down on the wedge of sofa at right angles to their own block of seat. But he could feel the tension of the man's body, poised for shock or for flight.

'Yes, I see that, but why should you want to see *me?*' asked Innes, leaning forward and frowning. His hands hung loosely between his knees, but Peter saw that they were trembling. 'I mean, I didn't know the man.'

'Your friend Annabel Gordon knew him,' said Peter, hoping his smile, too, was reassuring. 'And we know from Mrs Trent herself that you appeared briefly at a dinner party at which she was present and at which Miss Gordon also put in an appearance. We're contacting everyone, Mr Innes, who is known to have had any kind of contact with Charles Hugo Stratton in the weeks before his death, however casually. So often this is the way evidence is corroborated.'

'I only saw Stratton one other time. The day after that dinner party.' Innes paused.

'Yes?' encouraged Peter, allowing his interested surprise to appear in moderated form in his face.

'I went to see him, actually.' Yes, thought

Peter, Annabel Gordon would know that, and might have told. And the woman charged with the murder might have told of Innes's pursuit of Miss Gordon, and his anger, the night of the dinner party. 'I felt... Annabel Gordon, my girlfriend, had got a bit obsessed with him, and frankly–' as if in illustration of his frankness, warming to his theme, Innes for the first time looked Peter and then Geoff in the eye, confident, almost animated – 'I blamed him for it.'

'Why?' asked Peter, trying to sound like a man slightly intrigued by the doings of a friend.

'Well...' Again, briefly, Innes frowned. 'He has – had–' the hands now were trembling so strongly they had to grip one another in order to steady themselves – 'a very strong personality and ... and ... he tended to use it to attract – people – to him. And then, if he got bored, he just didn't bother.' Although Innes was still looking them alternately in the eye, Peter realized that he now appeared even more ill than when he had come up to them, his white face shining with sweat.

He judged it time for an intervention. 'And you felt this was what he had done with Miss Gordon?'

'Yes. She was very unhappy,' responded Innes almost eagerly. 'She'd done quite a lot of good photographic work with – Stratton, and of course I wasn't objecting to that, but

I did want a word with him about the personal hot and cold which was upsetting Annabel so much.'

'I can understand that. And,' continued Peter, smiling, 'that you were a little bit jealous of him, as well.'

The one thing he hadn't expected was the look of astonishment. But it changed so fast into an expression of meek acceptance he wondered if perhaps he had imagined it. 'Yes,' said Roger Innes, coldly smiling. 'Of course I was jealous. But if I'd been Annabel's brother I'd still have called on him.'

'Good for you!' supplied Geoff Hughes, as if admiration had wrung the exclamation out of him. 'So you offered a few home truths.'

Elaborately Innes shrugged, and with that gesture somehow lost Peter's belief in him. 'I said what I felt I had to say. Stratton wasn't the sort of man who would ever let you see if you got to him. He – listened to me.' Playing it by ear, as Innes was playing it now?

'And then?' asked Geoff, another interested friend.

'Then I left. He – didn't come back at me, he didn't lose his temper, so when I'd said my say all I could do was go.' Innes's face, now, was very pale pink, and his breathing was noticeable.

'We appreciate you telling us all this, Mr

Innes. Did you visit Mr Stratton again? See him again?'

'No. As I said, that was the only time. I'm sorry.'

'Ah!' Peter tinged his smile with disappointment bravely borne. 'There it is, then. I was going to ask you if by any remote chance you had seen Mrs Trent on the day of Mr Stratton's death arriving either at Belmont Gardens, or actually at the door of his flat, somewhere between half past twelve and one, but there'd be no point.'

'I'm afraid not, Inspector.' Roger Innes's hands were tightly clasped.

'Chief Inspector,' murmured Detective-Sergeant Hughes.

'Right you are, Mr Innes, we won't take up any more of your time. We're more grateful than we can say for all your frankness and cooperation.'

'Well, of course, Chief Inspector,' said Roger Innes almost cheerfully. Peter noticed him separate his hands and place them lightly on his knees, where they lay still. But this was a member of the trio who couldn't possibly be questioned any further. And a member whose photograph WPC Elaine Mitchell would show to the porter at Belmont Gardens as the photograph of the brother she was trying to contact, whom someone she knew thought they'd seen going into the block of flats – could he possibly be an angel and tell her whether in fact the man in the photograph lived there or visited regularly?'

They were a self-absorbed threesome, thought Peter as he and Geoff passed appreciatively into the fresh air. Not one of them had taken the opportunity of questioning him about Mrs Trent. And only one of them, if the Chief Superintendent's instructions turned out to fit the facts, could be consciously steering clear of any comment on the woman who had so miraculously saved him or her from suspicion.

CHAPTER 11

'Oh, Sam, you always look so *cool!*' protested the small, plump, perspiring young woman as she sat heavily down in the vacant chair at the table for two.

'I don't let myself get flustered,' responded Samantha de Vere, not as any sort of reproof for the air of disorganization which almost always surrounded her friend Mandy, merely as an accurate statement of her own admirable self-control. 'Try moving more slowly,' she offered after a few moments' contemplation of Mandy's rosy face and heaving breast.

'But I'm always late so I have to hurry!' explained Mandy breathlessly.

Samantha shrugged. 'Start earlier in the morning,' she suggested. 'Get everything ready the night before, like I do.'

'Oh, I couldn't be like *you*, Sam,' responded Mandy vigorously. 'I mean... This awful business over your friend Hugo, you've been so *wonderful*. I could never... How do you feel, Sam? *Really?*'

Mandy leaned across the table, her hand wandering above the condiments in its desire to lay itself over Samantha's and press

184

it consolingly. But both Samantha's hands were out of sight on her lap.

'Yes?' snapped the waitress, suddenly beside them.

Each girl ordered a beefburger and a coffee, and the waitress passed on to the table just beyond them, where another girl, who was sitting on her own, asked for coffee and a Danish pastry.

'How do you feel, Sam, really?' pursued Mandy doggedly, the instant the waitress was gone.

'I think I'd rather not talk about it.' Samantha's beautiful mouth drew in slightly.

'Oh yes, Sam, of course.'

For five or ten minutes Mandy talked about her office politics, her workmates, and her gorgeous new boss, Samantha de Vere giving no indication of whether or not she found the disjointed statements interesting. Or whether or not she was listening to them. Eventually Mandy leaned for the second time across the table.

'When I asked you how you felt, Sam, I was only really meaning, what do you think about this Mrs Trent who ... who... I mean, you met her, did she seem – strange?'

Samantha de Vere made a nestling movement in her chair. 'I thought she was odd. Not just because she was a foreigner.'

'Odd?' coaxed Mandy.

'Two beefburgers!' The waitress set the

plates sharply in front of them. 'Two coffees!' She moved on to the next table.

'Odd?' questioned Mandy again.

'Yeah.' If Samantha was annoyed by her friend's questions, her face didn't show it. 'Sort of intense. Clever-clever.'

'That's what you said once about Hugo,' took up Mandy eagerly. 'You said to me once, Hugo's a bit clever-clever.'

'Did I? I don't remember. He and Mrs Trent weren't alike. Not a bit. I couldn't see why...' Samantha leaned over her plate as she loaded her fork with bun and beef.

'Couldn't see why what, Sam?'

'Why Hugo asked her opinion all the time. There was nothing special about her.' Samantha very slightly frowned. 'She was just – odd.'

'But, Sam...' Mandy swallowed a large mouthful the wrong way, and had to drink half her cup of coffee before she could stop coughing. 'There must have been something... I mean, for her to have *killed* him, and then got in touch with the police!'

'She was odd, I told you.' Samantha took a sip of coffee. 'I'm not all that surprised.'

'That she murdered him? Or that she rang the police?'

Samantha stared across the table. 'Both,' she said eventually. She put a small forkful of food into her mouth, glanced at her friend's already shiningly empty plate, then

186

at her wristwatch. 'I thought you were meeting your mother at seven.'

'Heavens, yes!' Mandy drained her coffee-cup. 'Come to the station with me, Sam?'

'I think I'll just take my time finishing this and maybe have another cup of coffee. Then I'll go home. I've told Frank I'll go back to the hotel tonight, he's got some special clients, and I want to wash my hair first.'

'You *are* good, Sam,' said Mandy admiringly. 'Will you stay the night?'

'Frank's put a room at my disposal. He won't let me work in the evenings unless I agree to stay, he says the streets and public transport are too dangerous at nights now for him to have the responsibility of letting me go home alone after dark.'

'You *are* lucky, Sam, to have such a great boss. My new chap's great, too, but I can't imagine him… Heavens, I'd better dash.'

'If you'd left ten minutes ago,' said Samantha, with her first slight smile since Mandy had sat down, 'you could have gone more slowly.'

'Oh *Sam!*' Mandy puffed to her feet, out of breath at the mere prospect of another breakneck journey.

'You can leave me your share of the bill if you like,' said Samantha, glancing down at the menu. 'Save yourself a bit of time. Eighty-five p.'

'Thanks, Sam.' Mandy rummaged ener-

187

getically in her large, heavy handbag, and found the right coins. 'Will I see you tomorrow?'

'I don't know what I'm doing tomorrow,' said Samantha. 'I'll give you a ring round about lunch-time.'

'That'll be great, Sam. I'm on the switchboard tomorrow. Have a good evening!'

In a whirl of packages she was gone, and Samantha signalled the waitress.

'Another coffee, please, and a chocolate éclair.'

The girl at the next table secured the waitress as she was turning away, and asked for her bill. The waitress wrote it out and handed it to her, and the girl got to her feet.

Only to collapse, moaning, on to the chair just vacated by Mandy.

'Cramp,' she groaned into Samantha's scarcely inquiring face as she jerked off a shoe and leaned down to pull her toes towards her. 'I keep getting it at the moment, it's been so bad I've made an appointment with the doctor. Mind if I just sit here for a moment and let it subside? I'm so sorry to bother you.'

'That's all right,' conceded Samantha, expressionless.

'Thanks.' Elaine grinned. 'It can be awfully embarrassing sometimes, especially when one's in the middle of being intense, or trying to make an impression. D'you ever get it?'

'Now and then. In bed, mostly.'

The waitress put a large chocolate éclair in front of Samantha, with a cup of coffee beside it.

'Could I have a glass of water, please, do you think?' Elaine asked her.

'Water?' repeated the waitress, in cold incredulity.

'Yes. I've got cramp. Sometimes it's caused by dehydration and a glass of water–'

'A glass of water!' The waitress stalked away.

'Do forgive me,' said Elaine, 'but I'm trying to take my mind off my foot – if I just sit waiting for another spasm it tends to come – and I'm looking at your nail varnish. It's such a super colour. Well, of course, you've got such super nails, any colour would look good. But that particular shade, I'm always looking for it and never finding it.' There was no doubt the beautiful eyes opposite were staring at the small unvarnished squares of Elaine's fingernails, but there was nothing showing in the face of the surprise Samantha de Vere must surely be experiencing at the thought of their owner bothering to put colour of any kind on such workmanlike appendages, let alone of a particular shade.

'Red-'n-gold,' conceded Samantha. 'It's made by Supa Products, a new company. You can get it at that big chemist just along the road, but not usually at the smaller ones.

It's only been going a few weeks.'

'Thanks,' effused Elaine. 'Thanks awfully.' She straightened up, smiling in surprise. 'It's worked, you see, the cramp's all gone. It often does when I can stop thinking about it.'

'You haven't had your glass of water,' said Samantha with slight sternness, as if the cramp had no right to take itself off until Elaine had dealt with it according to plan.

'I know, but I don't think I need it now. Have you noticed how almost impossible it is to get a glass of water in a restaurant? It doesn't matter how efficient the service is for everything else, you almost always have to ask twice, or even three times, for a glass of water.'

'No, I don't think I've noticed,' said Samantha.

'I wonder if my boyfriend will go for that Red-and-gold,' said Elaine, feeling the blush at her apparent idiocy creeping up her neck. 'Does your boyfriend like it on you?'

'I've never asked,' said Samantha composedly, studying Elaine's face for the first time, and no doubt seeing it flood with colour. She'd made a fool of herself for nothing and the only good thing about it was that there was obviously no use whatsoever carrying on acting like one. She'd heard Miss de Vere give nothing away to her friend, and if she wasn't prepared to confide in a devoted acolyte she was scarcely likely to talk to a stranger. It was really only her obsessive devotion to duty, thought Elaine ruefully as she eased her foot back into her shoe, which had made her carry on into an even more unpromising situation. All that effort, she continued to herself as she got up from Miss de Vere's table, smiling inwardly as well as on the surface because she could never take herself entirely seriously, and all she had really succeeded in doing was to lay bare a non-existent personality. And, at least, gain a consistent impression of Samantha de Vere's self-control.

On her way to the paydesk she caught sight of the waitress advancing across the café with nothing in her hand but a glass of water, and turned her back cravenly on the indignant figure.

Detective Chief Inspector Peter Hewitt, wearing blue jeans and a heavy round medal to fill the long angle of his half open shirt, strolled into the disco a few moments after Annabel Gordon and her escort. His frame of mind, he realized, matched his appearance: it was inappropriately youthful. He'd had a surprisingly easy time tracking her to a place where he was going to be able to speak to her – she'd come out of her flat when he'd only been hanging about for ten minutes, and the young man she had met in the pub along the road hadn't been Roger Innes and wasn't, obviously, at this stage any more than an acquaintance. They'd stayed for the length of a drink which he'd been glad of, himself, after a difficult day (the pub was old and convoluted, and he was certain they hadn't seen him drinking his single whisky round a corner), and then slowly walked the couple of blocks to the disco, where he'd seen them go in.

So the stage had been easily set, and the rest of his sense of euphoria and adventure came from the adrenalin which always flowed on those rare occasions he worked incognito. It fitted in with his mood, too, that Annabel Gordon was so very much his physical type.

Detective-Sergeant Geoff Hughes had wanted to come with him, and he had thought about it quite carefully before deciding to come on his own. Two people together were always more conspicuous than one alone, there was double the scope for distinguishing features, and there was also the overall impression created by a pair – in this case, tall and short – which Peter always thought trebled the possibility of being memorable. Now, as he stood in the entrance to the arena, blinking at the turning strobes, surreptitiously pushing cotton wool into his ears, he was glad to be on his own.

'You like to dance?'

The small girl with the minimal amount of

fair hair on her narrow skull was speaking to him, had asked her question twice before he recalled that he had attired himself in a way to invite such an approach. He was still, despite his agreeable sense of secrecy and relaxation, primarily a policeman.

'Yeah,' he said, and followed her into the intermittent gloom.

The cotton wool helped a bit, but he still found the noise uncomfortably loud, while the violent alternations of light and dark hurt his eyes. So much for his current image, grinned Peter Hewitt, and must have let his amusement show, because the girl gyrating in front of him yelled the question of what was so funny.

'I was just thinking,' blinked Peter apologetically, bending with reluctance towards one of the small ears which he found almost alarmingly obtrusive on the near naked head, 'how odd it all is, just standing here, moving about... Don't worry,' he encouraged, as a vague alarm broke the blank surface of the face, 'I'm crazy. But harmless.' He grinned again.

The child shrugged and continued in front of him until the noise came to an end. Then muttered something, slipped into the throng, and was instantly lost. Shrugging in his turn, Peter started moving slowly in the direction of the bar, his eyes out for Annabel Gordon.

His luck was holding. She was sitting alone almost in a corner, staring down at the glass table in front of her as she traced a finger round one of the numerous sticky rings on its surface.

Quick as a cat he was standing in front of that table.

'Hello,' he said. 'Please let me get you a drink.'

She looked up, swiftly and nervously, and stared at him for a few seconds before seeing him.

'Someone's getting me one,' she said, still regarding him. 'But thanks.'

Peter glanced at the packed crush of people which completely obscured his sight of the bar.

'Looks as though he'll be a bit of a time. We could dance and you could watch out for him.'

He waited, the adrenalin surging at its height, his fingers crossed against his tightly imprisoned denim thighs.

'All right,' she said, and got up and came round the table.

The music had moderated into a semblance of melody and dance rhythm, and he noticed one or two couples holding each other in the old-fashioned way. Venturing to do likewise and not being repulsed, he steered them quickly away from the fringes of the crowd, into its almost static heart.

'Hello,' he said again, as they stood face to face, forced close to one another by the press of people. 'Thank you for agreeing to dance with me.'

'For agreeing to go through the motions.' Irrelevant to his purpose, his heart leapt. One sentence had told him they were possibly on the same wavelength. 'One can't exactly dance in these conditions.'

'I'll settle for the motions.' How foreign to him, really, were the slick responses he had decided on before he had started to follow her?

She shrugged, losing the slight interest she had possibly been showing, but in the moment he was aware of his unprofessional reaction of regret he realized that he had played no part in his sudden loss of her attention, that it was caused by the return of the sombre mood out of which he had temporarily drawn her when he had stopped at her table.

'You're sad, aren't you?' he questioned softly, laying his cheek briefly close to the ear which, protected by a tangle of long dark hair, was in such reassuring contrast to the bare shell he had already approached that evening.

He drew back to observe the effect of his words in her face, and watched her eyes shorten their gaze from some far horizon to his own so close to them.

Briefly, wearily, she smiled. 'I'm sorry if it shows.'

She hadn't denied it.

'I'm sorry you're sad.'

He felt the shrug ripple between his hands. 'Anyone who'd never been sad, or frustrated, or disappointed, would be pretty poisonous, don't you think?'

'Heavens, yes!'

'Swings and roundabouts,' said Annabel Gordon, and Peter received the faint impression that she was sufficiently in control of her sorrow to be able to stand away from it and recognize it as something which might make her interesting. Certainly, when she looked in her mirror, she must see how it became her dark, intense style of beauty.

Could this exceptional young woman really have committed murder?

The Chief Superintendent had been informed that she could.

'I think perhaps you arrived here with someone tonight,' he whispered humbly. 'But will you please leave with *me?*'

He was aware of the effect of his plea on her body, which for a moment stood stock-still. Then, leaning back and giving herself again to the slight movement which was all he had room to inaugurate, she glanced with another brief smile over towards the bar.

'Hang on a moment,' she said, and slid away from him.

He might have panicked but he didn't, he felt he already knew Annabel Gordon well enough to be confident she wasn't a woman to be sidetracked once she had made up her mind. He followed her slowly, and when he was clear of the dance floor he saw her approaching the man she'd come in with, who appeared to be deeply absorbed with a girl whom a temporary rift in the press around the bar showed him to be blonde and animated.

He saw Annabel raise her hand to her head, make a vague gesture in his direction, smile and withdraw in the face of no more than a conventional show of concern.

She came straight back to him.

'There's only one thing,' she said into his ear. 'I'm afraid I'll have to leave now. I told Steve I had a headache and that an old friend I'd bumped into had offered to take me home.'

'No hard feelings?'

'Oh, none. Only a feeling of relief, that he can consolidate his meeting with that hard-working blonde.' Annabel Gordon spoke automatically, without rancour or any other emotion. 'You don't have to leave as well, of course.' She had started to walk towards the exit.

'I'm quite pleased to leave. I haven't been here before and it's too crowded and noisy.' He put his hand on the shoulder in front of him, to offset the deliberate casualness of his words. 'The only thing is,' he said on the step, in his normal voice, 'that I can't run you home. I didn't come by car.'

He welcomed her third smile. 'I only live along the road.'

'So may I walk you home?' He'd leave open until the last possible moment the chance that she would be the one to suggest prolonging the acquaintance beyond the entrance to the building where she lived.

She shrugged again, and he remembered how it had felt. 'If you like.'

It was a fine mild evening, and as he strolled beside her he was aware not only of his health and strength, but also of a sort of childlike awareness of the immediate moment which to his slightly shamefaced surprise he found headily refreshing.

'I live here,' she said, too soon. 'You didn't have a drink at the disco,' she went on, after a pause in which they looked at one another and he opened his mouth to start inviting himself into her flat. 'Would you like one now?'

'I'd like a coffee,' he said. 'Thanks.' His relief, his absurd sense of triumph, was shot through with dismay that she should be asking a total stranger to enter her home. Perhaps, before leaving, he could warn her against such behaviour without exciting any suspicions. Her action, though, was no doubt part of that indifference to the present which he knew from his own experience to be an aspect of sexual despair.

She preceded him in silence up a quite elegant flight of shallow stairs. This had to be expensive accommodation. *Only child, father and mother extant, father a stockbroker in the City.* Reluctantly his photographic memory recalled the sentence from half way down the A4 printout.

Immediately behind her front door was a large hall-living-room attractively and minimally furnished. On a table in a prominent position was a photograph of Charles Hugo Stratton.

'Oh!' he said, as anyone who read the papers would surely have said, making a move towards the photograph which he checked when he had almost reached it. 'I'm sorry, but I recognized...'

'Yes,' she said, passing him to pick the photograph up. 'Yes. Hugo was my lover. I feel as if I'm dead, too.'

'I'm sorry,' said Peter. 'If I'd known I wouldn't have...'

'With that woman giving herself up,' said Annabel, 'nobody had to know. At least she spared me the publicity.'

'I'm so sorry.' Almost he repeated himself, but his meaning now was different, he was expressing his sorrow for her, rather than for his own behaviour. 'How absolutely terrible for you. You needn't have been polite, asking me in. The last thing you must want now is to have to pretend to feel like company...'

It was a fearful gamble, but if it came off he was home and dry, and he thought it would come off.

'Actually, it can help. How do you like your coffee?'

'Khaki-coloured. Thanks. I'd like to stay a bit. Can I help? Or hinder?'

The euphoria was back as he followed her out to her small, idiosyncratically attractive kitchen. He knew she would allow him to touch her, if only because she would be unable to feel it, but he didn't of course try, he perched on a stool and watched her as she made coffee and put some healthy-looking biscuits on the tray with the coffee-pot and two hand-thrown beakers. He carried the tray back into the big room.

'Yes,' she said, when she had poured them both coffee and thrown herself down in a chair. 'I loved Hugo, and he loved me. It's what's commonly called a tragedy.'

She smiled at him bravely, and attacked a biscuit.

'I'm not going to ask you to talk about it, of course,' said Peter warily. 'But there's just one thing that puzzles me. And a large part of the population of the British Isles, no doubt. Why did that Mrs Talbot ... Tench...'

'Trent,' supplied Annabel Gordon.

'Why did that Mrs Trent kill him? And then send for the police? I know that we'll be offered a reason or reasons when she comes to trial, but at the moment it's a mystery and I can't resist–'

'I don't know,' said Annabel. Her green eyes appeared to be looking candidly into his. 'I don't know. All I know is that she and her husband are – were–' she blinked and he saw her eyes suddenly sparkle as tears invaded them – 'old friends of Hugo's, he often spoke about them, especially about her, he thought very highly of her.'

'You've met her, of course?' He drained his beaker. The coffee was very good.

'Just once, when…' For the first time since he had spoken to her she was really faltering. 'It was quite briefly, once. But I liked her right away, she seemed the last person who would – commit a murder. But she confessed to it, didn't she?' She was looking straight at him again. 'So I suppose she must have killed Hugo, although I can't begin to imagine it, or why she did.'

'Yes, I suppose she must. I'm so sorry,' he said yet again. 'It must be like a nightmare for you.'

'Like a nightmare,' she repeated. 'Yes.' Suddenly, and to his horror rather than the objective interest which ought to have been his reaction, her face broke up into an ugly, sobbing despair which she made no attempt to control or disguise.

'Hugo didn't love me!' she shouted across to him. 'I was only pretending he did because I loved him and that was what I wanted to believe. I thought if I said it often enough, to myself and to other people who didn't know the truth, I might eventually believe it, but of course I can't. I've never been any good at self-deception. We were lovers once, for a short time, and we were friends until I spoiled it. In the end I made Hugo loathe the sight of me.' Her face now was blotched red and white, tears shone on her cheeks and her mouth when she paused rose in the distorted arc of weeping grief. 'The last thing he said to me, the last time I saw him—'

'Don't say it!' urged Peter. 'Don't even think of it!'

He couldn't say whether he had made another tactical move, or given in to his sense of compassion.

Annabel Gordon had either not heard him, or was undeflectable until she had completed her confession. 'He said, "To be absolutely honest, darling, you have become a quite insupportable bore." That was the last thing Hugo Stratton said to me!'

So that all that was left for you to do was to kill him?

The question formed on a reflex in the detective chief inspector's brain, but his emotions were still a mélange of pity and attraction, and he dropped on his knees from his low chair to put his arms round Annabel Gordon's heaving shoulders.

'It's all right,' he murmured, 'it's all right.'

He tried to lift her hair back from her face, and to raise her head with a hand beneath her chin, but with the end of her revelation her self-respect had returned and he knew she was ashamed of her appearance as well as her performance.

He didn't know if she had come to the end of her story, but he knew it had gone as far as she was going to take it. He knew too, as gradually he overcame the hostility which had followed her disclosure of her humiliation, that he could have stayed with her till the morning. He didn't have any real struggle to get up and leave when he judged she was sufficiently recovered to be on her own – even if he had been with her as his private self he would never have accepted the hospitality of a bed offered out of indifference. If she had wanted him to stay he didn't know what he would have done, but as that situation was academic, he didn't have to look for the answer to it.

CHAPTER 12

Roger Innes didn't walk as steadily into the second pub as he'd walked into the first.

Detective-Inspector Bob Ryan drove himself and Detective-Sergeant Johnny Boyle round to the pub car park, where he found it difficult to tell Johnny that he thought a stage had been reached where Innes had become a proposition for one man rather than two.

'However, the odds must still be against finding myself in a position to give him a lift home,' he concluded. 'And/or I may need to call on you. I'm certain he wasn't aware of us at the last place. Follow me in in a few minutes and have a drink where you can see us if not hear us. But ideally both.'

Bob Ryan got out of the car and went round the pseudo-Tudor building into the saloon bar. It was eight o'clock in a prestigious London village and the pre-dinner drinkers were only just giving way to the ones who ate first. He spotted Innes at once, already solitarily and conveniently ensconced in a corner with the fourth double whisky and water Bob had seen him drink that evening. His table was quite near to the bar, and from the position Bob took up leaning casually against the counter he could watch Innes in close-up, the more easily as the whisky had obviously already taken him beyond the stage of full awareness of his surroundings. He sat hunched into himself, his eyes staring unseeingly across the table top, inert but for the frequent movement of his hand to his mouth and an occasional shudder which seemed to shake his whole body.

When he'd received and paid for his half-pint of bitter, Bob surveyed the comfortable and characterless saloon bar and was gratified to observe that each table had an occupant. Not, again, that Roger Innes was in any state to suggest to someone sitting down at his table that there was an empty one elsewhere, but it was always more satisfactory if official actions were able to appear totally natural. Slowly, nodding to the landlord as he turned away, Bob Ryan made his way towards Roger Innes.

'Mind if I take the weight off my feet?'

He had to ask the question twice, and was already sitting down when Innes eventually looked up at him.

'Do' mind, no.' Innes's glance lengthened again, to somewhere in the vicinity of Johnny Boyle, who was leaning against the bar counter not much beyond the spot where Bob had lately been standing. Innes,

Bob was sure, didn't see Johnny.

But the next moment, with that sudden detailed concentration which is the unnerving obverse of drunken vagueness, Innes had seized Bob's arm, making him jump, and was looking earnestly into his face.

'Need to talk to someone,' said Innes.

'Sure,' responded Bob, slightly out of breath with the shock of his good fortune. 'Here, or somewhere else?'

Innes, with a gesture almost of revulsion, let go of Bob's sleeve. 'Oh, here. I'm not going outside with you.' He was trying to keep his eyes steady on Bob's face, an expression in his own of knowing suspicion. It couldn't be, though, that he knew why Bob was there. 'I'm not going outside with any man,' stressed Innes, in what struck Bob as a peculiar turn of phrase.

'Talk away if it will help,' he said sympathetically.

Innes drained his glass. 'Nothing'll help. 'Cept another drink.' He wasn't touting, he was merely stating what he saw at that moment as his prime need, but Bob was on his feet.

'I'll get it. Have another myself.'

'Know him?' he asked the man behind the bar, looking indulgently back at Innes.

'Never seen him in my life,' said the man as he carefully poured Bob's bitter. 'And it's my pub. Looks as though I'll have to start keeping an eye on him soon. Reckon events must have sent him on a crawl.'

Carrying the drinks back to the table, Bob Ryan reckoned that the landlord was right. He'd conferred on the telephone with Detective Chief Inspector Hewitt before setting out, to see if anything had been learned from Innes officially, and heard about his self-confessed visit to Stratton shortly before Stratton's death. It would be something of a coincidence if another cataclysmic event in addition to the murder of Stratton had also laid a finger on Innes, although his devastation now, of course, might indicate no more than a connection at a remove – such as the defection of his girlfriend Annabel Gordon as a consequence of Stratton's death.

'Here we are!' Bob Ryan put the whisky in front of Innes, went back to the counter and brought the jug of water. 'Say when.'

'Tha's enough.' Innes spoke at once, but Bob didn't at once stop pouring, he didn't want Innes totally incoherent.

'Now,' he said gently, when he had sat down again, 'what's the trouble?'

'Trouble? Trouble?' Innes stared at him in angry disbelief. 'You call it trouble, one's whole way of life in jep ... jep ... jeopardy?' He pushed the word out quickly, just getting it right. 'Trouble, not to know any more what ... what... what one is? Well, it is trouble, I suppose, big trouble. Like having a hormone implant.' Innes gave an unpleasant-sounding snicker of laughter, and Bob glanced up and caught Johnny Boyle's eye.

'I don't quite understand,' encouraged Bob.

'Neither do I!' The anger in the dark eyes didn't altogether mask the plea for help. 'Don't unnerstand at all, unnerstand nothing any more. Not unnerstanding oneself, now that's something. What? What?'

Again, with that sudden unnerving switch, Innes was exclusively and impatiently aware of Bob Ryan, and demanding a reaction.

'Must be terrible,' agreed Bob cautiously.

''Tis.' Innes removed his eyes to the distance, for the moment appearing to be satisfied. 'Couldn't tell you... Fr'instance, might find that *you...*' He surveyed Bob again, but this time as if he was a picture on a wall or a model in a shop window, not expected to respond. 'No,' went on Innes, shaking his head, 'no. Not you. But someone, could be someone. Don't *know*. Could be *him*.' He pointed a finger in the direction of Johnny Boyle, who casually turned his attention to his beer glass on the bar counter. 'Don't *know*.' All at once Innes was struggling to his feet. 'Get us 'nother drink.'

'It's all right, I'll get them.'

Innes flopped back on to the bench.

'A'right. But my turn. My money.' He put a tense restraining hand on Bob Ryan's arm, then withdrew it in the same way he had withdrawn it the first time, as if he had been stung. 'Here… Take this. Must…'

The five pound note was scratching the side of his hand, and Bob took hold of it. 'Thanks,' he said. 'Just hang on now.' He walked the few steps to the bar. 'I'll try to make it his last,' he told the landlord. 'And I'll try to take him home. Advisable if he didn't come by car, essential if he did.' They grinned at one another, sharing the righteous glow that surrounds two sober men in the presence of a drunken third. Bob extended his own grin to include Johnny.

''Evening. Stand by,' he murmured to the bar counter, as the landlord turned his back. 'By the end of this one I don't think he'll notice a second party.'

'No water,' said Innes, when Bob had managed to pour out a few drops. He kept pulling his hand away when Bob went to put the change into it, but eventually seemed to realize what Bob was trying to do and stuffed the coins into a pocket. 'Cheers!' Innes raised his glass, drank half its contents, and waveringly replaced it on the table. 'Can't get away,' he murmured into it. 'Can't get away from oneself. Stuck there. A cage. We're all in cages. Every one of us. Bu' mostly we don't notice.' Bob Ryan's fingers itched for his notebook, and Johnny wasn't quite within earshot. He tried to print Innes's ramblings on his brain as Innes picked up his glass again, lifted it to his lips, drained it, and set it carefully down.

Then slowly, almost gracefully, he slumped forward on to the table, pushing the glass ahead of him until his head was resting on his arms.

On a reflex Bob Ryan saved the glass from falling off the far side of the table, then spent a few seconds accepting that Roger Innes had drunk himself into temporary oblivion. Both Johnny Boyle and the landlord were watching.

'He's out,' explained Bob at the counter. 'If we can find his address on him – for obvious reasons I don't want to look for it on my own – I'll run him home so long as he doesn't live in Hull or Birmingham.'

Innes's address, of course, was something which *was* imprinted on his brain, but there must be nothing left from this small incident to go on teasing the brain of the pub's landlord once he and Johnny had taken Innes away.

'Good idea,' responded the landlord quickly, brightening. Bob and Johnny in fact stood back while he went through Innes's pockets until he found a wallet. There was a driving licence in it.

'Roger Innes, 9 Harcourt Gardens,

SW10,' read out the landlord. 'Not too far out of your way?' he asked Bob hopefully.

'That's fine.' Bob turned to Johnny. 'Perhaps you'd be kind enough to give me a hand with him out to my car?'

'Sure. I'll help you get him home if it isn't a two-seater.'

'It isn't. Thanks.'

Gratefully declining the landlord's offer to help Innes off his premises, Bob and Johnny took his slight weight between them with the ease of experience, bore him swiftly out of and round the pub and laid him on the back seat of the car, making sure both rear doors were locked even though there was no doubt that at that moment Innes was incapable of attempting to open one.

'Something's bugging him badly,' observed Johnny, looking down at Innes after he had taken his bunch of keys. Even the hard-won oblivion wasn't clearing the anxiety from the thin white face.

'I should say so.' Before starting the car Bob quickly wrote down what he could remember of Innes's enigmatic pronouncements. On a tacit agreement to say nothing in that confined space which could make a reviving Innes suspicious, Johnny made no comment.

Bob had expected the usual parking difficulties and an unwelcome long drag from the car, but Innes's place turned out to be a mansion flat in one of those early Victorian stuccoed crescents which provide both an inner and an outer ring of roadside, and there was a space quite near.

His second exposure to fresh air left Innes as limp between the two policemen as he had been on their way out of the pub, and with a glance at Bob at the foot of the first flight of stairs, Johnny hoisted the relaxed body over his shoulder as if it was an unstrung puppet, and was still able to keep up with his superior officer on that flight and the next.

On the second landing he propped Innes against the wall while Bob Ryan opened his front door.

'Bring him in, Johnny,' said Bob softly, still aware, after eight or nine years of uninvited entry, of a sense of trespass which always disturbed him as he failed in his efforts to suppress it.

He moved quickly through the flat, settling for the larger of the two bedrooms where the bed had wrinkled pillows and duvet and there were some clothes on a chair. Johnny laid Innes on his back and the two policemen stood looking down at him.

'Totally out,' murmured Bob Ryan, after lifting an eyelid. 'He was exhausted before he started.' He took Johnny by the arm and led him back to the door. 'It's a chance we've got to take, it's too good to pass up on. And Elaine just might not be able to get in – pity we haven't got any wax. You stay here with him while I go round the rest of the flat.'

It was all quite clean and tidy, and without any real evidences of a personality, as though Innes didn't feel settled in the place, that he was treating it as a no-man's-land between one phase of his life and another. There were one or two familiar and agreeable prints on the distempered sitting-room walls, expensively serviceable tables and comfortable chairs which were the right size for the space available, but nothing to suggest what it was in life that Innes found important.

Nor was there anything revealing in the few drawers, either in the sitting-room or the other small bedroom. The contents were neatly arranged and almost totally uninteresting. The only things, in fact, over which Bob paused were a stack of paper which, investigated, appeared to be an attempt to write a comedy series for television, a few personal but scarcely informal letters in a rack on the desk top, and a large photograph of Annabel Gordon upside down at the bottom of a desk drawer. The photograph had been placed tidily under the few other contents of the drawer, its glass was intact, its surface pristine, it hadn't been the victim of any uncontrollable attack of rage or jealousy, Innes had merely decided that he didn't want to look at it any longer...

The walk-in cupboard in the hall took the

most time, because of being the only place which was crowded with belongings, but there was nothing remotely of interest and the white powder Bob applied to his tongue turned out to be salt. In the spare bedroom the few drawers were empty except for a small bottle of indigestion tablets and a packet of 3-amp fuses. The bathroom cupboard held nothing he wouldn't have expected to see, and nothing to make him suddenly suspicious of the state to which six double whiskies had reduced Roger Innes.

That state was still unchanged when Bob Ryan went back into the larger bedroom. Even so he beckoned Johnny over to the door.

'Nothing anywhere. Everything rather tidy. Impersonal. A bit depressing, somehow.' He realized that as he spoke. 'Go back now, Johnny, and sit close to him while I have a look round in here.'

There was a built-in cupboard and an old-fashioned mahogany chest of drawers – the one piece of furniture, thought Bob Ryan, which might have some reference to Innes's earlier life. The cupboard revealed no more than hanging space and a few open shelves holding shirts and sweaters. In the three drawers were handkerchiefs, socks, underwear.

Except in the bottom drawer, where underneath some more pullovers he felt an irregular wadge of paper and cardboard.

Pulling it carefully out, Bob stood with Johnny Boyle's substantial body between him and Innes while he examined it.

Each piece was a photograph, the cardboard pieces studio portraits, the pieces of paper cuttings from newspapers and magazines.

Every photograph was of Charles Hugo Stratton.

Bob Ryan stared on a wild surmise at his detective-sergeant before bending down to rebury the photographs at the bottom of the open drawer and then moving back to the bed to look down at Roger Innes's sleeping face and see it in an entirely different light.

'Hello!' WPC Elaine Mitchell greeted the green-uniformed porter breathlessly, realizing as she spoke that she was using Samantha de Vere's disorganized friend as a model. 'I wonder if I could ask you an enormous favour?'

'Depends,' responded the porter, his face more promising than his voice. Elaine was glad he was elderly. This ought to preclude any sexual element in the concession she was hoping he would grant her, and should also make it more likely that he would take events on their merits rather than apply some overall policy in which he had been indoctrinated.

'Of course,' she said humbly, allowing herself to sound slightly chastened. 'It's just… I'm trying to get in touch with my brother. I know it sounds ridiculous, but there was a bit of a family quarrel and we haven't heard from him for a few weeks. Our mother's awfully worried, as you can imagine.' At least he was prepared to listen. 'Anyway, I think I've got a clue, but it all depends on you.' Elaine smiled at him in the way she still smiled at her father when she wanted a particular favour.

'Well, now,' said the porter, 'I reckon it would be a good idea if you told me what I can do. Not that I can imagine how I could possibly–'

'A friend of mine thought he caught sight of him a few days ago. Here. He was following him, and saw him go inside this block of flats. He'd have hung around if he possibly could have but he had an appointment and couldn't wait. Anyway…' Elaine paused and gulped. 'Here's a photograph of my brother–' she produced the excellent likeness of Roger Innes which the nameless ones who had given them the skimpy dossier must have taken somewhere on a London street – 'and I just wondered if you'd feel you could tell me whether you've ever seen him in here.'

Elaine waited, tense. This was the moment Detective Chief Inspector Hewitt had warned her was the dicey one. If this porter had been on duty the first time Roger Innes had entered the building in indignant pursuit of Annabel Gordon, he would have answered Innes's query as to the whereabouts of Charles Hugo Stratton's flat, and if he had any sort of a memory for faces he might now associate the photograph Elaine was holding out to him with the murder of the owner of one of the flats in his charge. If Roger Innes had asked the way a second time, he almost certainly would. But at least Mrs Trent had been the only person about whom the police had asked questions, and the public knew that she had been charged with the killing...

'Yes,' the porter was saying, 'I've seen that young chap.' No, he was making no connections, he had even decided to be on the young lady's side in her anxious quest for her brother.

'You have? Oh, that's marvellous!' Elaine hesitated. 'It would be too much to hope, I suppose, that you actually know who his contact is in the building?'

Thank goodness it was too much, or by now the man might have reached for his telephone.

'Afraid I don't know that, miss. But I can tell you I've definitely seen him – oh, must be about three or four times.'

'Three or four times,' mused Elaine. So at

last they were learning something.

'Not in the last few days,' pursued the porter. He studied the face she was struggling to make disappointed. 'Tell you what, you leave a note with me and I'll give it to him if he comes again. I can't exactly quit my desk here and follow him to see where he's going, you'll appreciate from my own point of view—'

'Of course not!' agreed Elaine. 'I wouldn't for the world expect you to. You've been such a help, I'm so grateful. I'll go off now and write him a letter.' She paused, thinking. The man was kind, and she didn't want to sour that kindness, however slightly. 'If you don't hear from me you'll know he's thought better of it of his own accord. Thanks *awfully!*'

Elaine whirled away on a smile of mingled victory and gratitude, but by the time she was back on the main road the sense of victory had given way to apprehension. The most difficult part of her unofficial assignment was still to come.

When the adrenalin flowed it made her hungry, and she took a sandwich with her into the telephone-box. They put her straight through to Peter Hewitt, he must have been waiting.

'Innes went to Belmont Gardens three or four times before Stratton's death, the porter was positive. Sorry, Governor, that's not why I'm telephoning, is it?'

'You'd have been less than human, Elaine, as well as remarkably silly, if you hadn't told me. Thanks. Now, Miss de Vere is at her hotel as usual today, Miss Gordon is filming a TV commercial and is hardly likely to get any sort of a midday break from *that*. Bob Ryan and Johnny Boyle can personally vouch for the fact that Roger Innes had a heavy night, but we've ascertained that he's managed to get to work this morning – and that won't give him any sort of a break long enough to come home in. Unless, of course, he finds himself unable to sustain the full working day, so I should begin with Innes if I were you. And look, Elaine, if you can't get into any of the places don't worry. No running the gauntlet of burglar alarms or tackling locks apart from simple Yales. With all three of them living in temporary kinds of accommodation, and being young and we hope comparatively careless, you mightn't come up against these hazards. But if you do, just leave it out and don't worry. See you at our meeting at five.'

'Thanks, Governor. I'll get going now.'

'Good girl.'

She had two hits and a miss, and it was just after four o'clock when she finished, having taken off no more than a quarter of an hour midday for another sandwich. At one of the places where she managed entry she was able to work at the simple lock from a corridor which offered her a good view each way and a fuse cupboard which she didn't have to use. At the other she had to hang about in the road because the main door opened only to a key or the pleasure of the tenant whose outside bell was rung. Elaine leaned against the wall just round the curve at the foot of the steps up to the door, reading a paperback book and hastening lazily up the steps as the door began to open from inside.

'Thanks awfully!' she said sweetly but firmly to the woman who was coming out, and had whirled authoritatively into the building before the woman was properly aware of her.

In neither place did she find anything which had a recognizable bearing on the murder of Charles Hugo Stratton, and there was only one thing which made her pause – an unlabelled cassette in a top drawer under some handkerchiefs, in a flat where there was no cassette-player.

Eventually she shut the drawer and went out of the flat leaving the front door un-latched.

The row of shops wasn't too far away, and was sufficiently diverse for Elaine to be able to buy a blank cassette, which she took straight back to the drawer containing the other one. They looked much the same, she thought, holding one in each hand, and she put the new one under the handkerchiefs, and the original one into her bag, before leaving the flat and clicking the Yale lock to behind her, trying to persuade herself that the reason she had taken the cassette – because there was nothing to play it on – was in favour of the flat's occupant not being immediately alerted to the substitution.

She'd noticed a rather good-looking pâtisserie on her way to buy the cassette, and she just had time for a coffee and a chocolate éclair before her meeting with what in her mind Elaine called the Team of the Elite.

CHAPTER 13

'Thank you, Samantha.' Frank Cannon tore the piece of paper he was holding into little pieces and showered them into the waste-paper basket on the floor by the desk. 'That's covered the correspondence for today, I think.' He took off his reading glasses and rubbed his eyes. He always looked sort of naked, Samantha thought, when he was what she called between glasses, almost sort of young. She had once or twice wondered if it was that little boy look of his, when she was about to be nice to him and his glasses were off, which made her just able to... Not tonight, though, not tonight. And probably not, she was beginning to think, any other night in the future.

Frank was feeling in his pockets for his distance pair.

'You ought to get yourself fixed up with bifocals.' Samantha found the glasses on the desk and handed them to him with the air of slight disapproval she knew he appreciated, because of its appearing to indicate that she was concerned about him. She would have done better to suppress it this evening, see-ing that she had decided to go home straight away, but it had become second nature.

'That's what everyone keeps telling me.' Everyone, Samantha knew, was Frank's fat bossy wife who never spent a night at the hotel and who only occasionally came there to give him a lift home if she happened to have been shopping in London. Mrs Cannon, believed Samantha, considered her husband's managership of the Miramar Hotel a sort of schoolboy hobby, to be treated with indulgent condescension. Before Samantha had begun to be nice to Frank he had called his wife by her name – that is, Mrs Cannon – in conversation with his secretary, and had confided the fact that she had money of her own. 'She's generous,' he had been wont to say, 'and she'd keep me. She wants to keep me, but I want to keep my independence. Well, I mean to say, Samantha.'

'Of course, Frank.'

Samantha had approved Franks attitude, she was all for independence whatever one's sex, but she adjudged her employer's wife to be unwisely complacent. When she, Samantha, eventually made her change of attitude known, there would be someone to fill the gap. Not that Frank was any sort of a sex maniac – Samantha sometimes thought it was merely the practical attraction of so many empty and anonymous bedrooms.

'No need to rush off, is there, Samantha?' Frank had pushed his chair back on to its

223

hind legs, his usual preliminary to bringing it firmly foursquare again and leaning over to pat her hand. The phrase *reculer pour mieux sauter* was not in Samantha's vocabulary, but it furnishes an exact description of her employer's invariable opening tactics at the end of the working day (and sometimes, depending on the overall circumstances, during it). He was a man of precise habit.

Now that the moment had recurred, Samantha saw that she might just have been prevailed upon to make it one more time, but tonight she had important things to think about, and she wanted to get the process under way. She wouldn't, though, close the door just yet. If she did, she would be almost bound to have to begin looking for another job, and she didn't feel quite strong enough to start on that particular slog.

'I wish there wasn't, Frank, but I'm meeting a friend in—' Samantha consulted the tiny gold watch Hugo had given her, which since his death seemed to be leaving a precise awareness of its dimensions against the skin of her wrist – 'less than an hour. Even if I tidy myself up here,' she went on, as quickly as she ever said anything, 'I'll still have to go straight off when I'm ready. Anyway, I want to change.'

She had always resisted, she didn't quite know why, Frank's constantly repeated suggestion that she build up a small wardrobe in one of the hotel bedrooms, so that she didn't always have to go home when she wanted to change. She hadn't even agreed to leave a dressing-gown hanging in one of the many tall thin cupboards, although she had got into the habit of carrying a toothbrush.

'A pity,' said Frank judicially, his chair teetering.

'I know. I really am sorry, but you wouldn't like me not to have a social life, especially when...'

Especially when you're not in a position to offer me one. The rest of Samantha's sentence had from the start been understood between them.

'Quite, dear, quite.' Frank gave a heavy sigh, but Samantha was confident his only reaction was the usual disappointment, that she had managed to withhold from him any suspicion of what she was moment by moment more certain was the imminent emptiness of his future so far as she was concerned. 'You've an interesting evening ahead of you, have you, then, Samantha?'

'Not especially. My friend Liz...'

Samantha saw her non-existent friend Liz far more often than she saw Mandy, or any other young woman of her acquaintance. 'She's a bit depressed at the moment, so I've said I'll go over for the night and maybe go with her to a disco.'

'I don't know that it's a good thing for two young girls on their own to go anywhere these days without an escort.' Frank had not been reassured by her description of her fictitious evening to come. (In one way he would have been happier to envisage the truth of the matter, that she would be spending the evening alone in her bedsitter, thinking, but at the same time he would have been unable to grasp that such a programme could possibly merit precedence over an hour or two in his company in one of the bedrooms of the Miramar Hotel.)

'Oh, we'll be all right. The disco Liz likes to go to is just round the corner from her flat.'

'Well, you both take care, anyway.' The argument in favour of an escort who could not be Frank himself was, as usual, quite speedily abandoned. 'Near Swiss Cottage, you said? That's where your friend Liz lives?'

'That's right.' Samantha got to her feet, finding it hard to suppress the usual provocation she brought to her movements. 'And now I think I'd better go, if that really is all the correspondence for today.'

'All I'll bother you with.' Samantha briefly smiled her acknowledgment of her employer's magnanimity. 'Off you go then, Samantha, and I'll see you in the morning.' Frank remained at his slight distance, making no move to bridge the gap between himself and his secretary. But with Frank Cannon, from the start, it had been all or nothing. Nothing in the office, beyond that acknowledging touch of the hand following Samantha's tacit agreement not to hurry away, and everything behind one of those uniform bedroom doors...

'I hope you haven't been cold, Samantha? You should have put the fire on.'

'That's all right.' Samantha's shiver had been involuntary. Not so much at the thought of Frank in one of his hotel bedrooms as at yet another stab of realization that Hugo was dead and that she would never again feel the dazzle of his presence. Being nice to Frank had been made easier by the wonderful knowledge that soon afterwards Hugo would be nice to *her*. One of the things she was going to have to think about when she got home, although not the main thing, was the solemn possibility that she might not be able to put anyone else in Hugo's place. 'Good night.'

At first, when she had begun being nice to Frank, Samantha had been a bit worried about living so close to the hotel, but she had soon learned that he was no more likely to come round to her flat (or to loiter about outside it – for a day or two she had peered regularly round her net curtain) than he was to approach her in the office.

It was a fine autumn evening, a slight mist

227

fragmenting the circular outlines of the street lights into stars, but Samantha, apart from being glad it wasn't raining, was unaware of the soft air on her cheek. As always, however, since she had realized that once she left the Miramar Hotel she no longer had to worry about Frank, she rejoiced in the good fortune of not having to plunge down into the rush-hour tube, of having merely to walk a few blocks of pavement. She couldn't hope to be lucky enough to get such a convenient job again... As soon as she got into her bedsitter – she had a bit of difficulty with her key into the Yale lock, but when she tried it a second time it seemed to be all right – she switched on her small oven, took the cardboard top off the foil carton of mariner's pie, changed her shoes, and turned on the television news. At least, now, they couldn't be saying anything terrible about Hugo.

There were things just about watchable on the television to take her through to the moment when the mariner's pie was ready, and before she sat down behind the small table on which she'd put her tray Samantha switched the television off and the radio on – quietly, just to cover the absolute silence. Then sat down, and with the first forkful of crispy mashed potato on its way to her mouth, began to think.

She thought of Detective Chief Inspector

Hewitt, dismissing her awareness of how attractive she had found him (perhaps, after all, eventually, she might be able to replace Hugo), and remembering his final words.

If there's anything else you feel might be helpful to us don't hesitate to get in touch.

She should have said it then, of course, but she hadn't been prepared. And she had said enough otherwise, they had been satisfied, they wouldn't be calling on her again.

So ought she to leave well alone, or should she go to them now and tell them the rest of it?

Don't hesitate to get in touch.

She couldn't see how they could actually *need* any evidence from her – she hadn't really been able to see in the first place why they had bothered to come and see her when Mrs Trent was already arrested and charged with Hugo's ... with the killing of Hugo, but on the other hand they had said they wanted to get every bit of evidence they could, so perhaps it would help the case against Mrs Trent if she, Samantha, told them that after all she was in a position to give them an eye-witness account of the murder, and had only held back through what she now saw was a misplaced sense of loyalty to another woman...

Samantha shivered, and got up to turn her gas fire on. It was an old one, and there was a small explosion as the gas ignited. When she had first left home and come to live in this dreary bedsitter that fire had scared the life out of her, and she had vowed then and there not to put up with it for long. She had seen Hugo, for that brief, wonderful time, as her deliverance from the fire and all the low-grade, second-rate things which made up the lives of low-grade second-rate people, but Hugo was dead.

Samantha sat down again, and picked up her fork.

One instinct was telling her to leave well alone, and the other was nagging at her that as she was in a position to give evidence against that Mrs Trent, the very thing the police had asked of her, she'd be a fool not to do it.

Don't pass up on your knowledge, said that instinct.

Don't overdo it, the other instinct advised her.

The conflicting advice was so muddling it was beginning to give her a headache, and Samantha got up a second time, to find a couple of aspirins and take them with a few sips of water at the sink.

By the time she sat down again she had made up her mind to sleep on the two possibilities. She'd done this before, the few times she'd been unable to make up her mind, and in the morning it had all come clear. When she woke up she would know whether or not to get in touch with that Detective-Inspector Hewitt.

From thoughts of Peter Hewitt it was a very little way to thoughts of the gap Hugo had left in the most important part of her life, and whether she really would ever be able to find another man to fill it. One thing she was sure of already: she wouldn't, now, be prepared to fill it with the low-grade and the second-rate, even as a temporary measure. Hugo had given her a standard, and from now on she would stay on her own rather than fall below it. That was why she didn't want to be nice to Mr Cannon any more; she didn't want another woman's husband unless he was worth permanently detaching, and she didn't want a man so much older than herself unless he was assured and attractive and had plenty of money and some sort of a position...

Oh, but Hugo! thought Samantha, on a sudden and unexpected pang of pain. It was a sensation so unusual she had to get up out of her chair and walk about the tiny room. There was no one like Hugo, with Hugo beside her she would never have wanted anyone or anything else in the world. Not just because of his charm and his wealth and his self-assurance. Even more than those things it was because he was himself. Because he was Hugo. Samantha realized, on an anguish which she was not equipped by nature to sustain, that she had loved him.

And he was dead.

It struck her, as she carried her empty plate out to the kitchenette and automatically squirted it with detergent, that when she had made up her mind in the morning what she was going to do, and had done it, probably the hardest thing she would have to contend with would be boredom.

'Here we are, then,' said Detective Chief Inspector Peter Hewitt as Detective-Inspector Bob Ryan and Detective-Sergeant Johnny Boyle came into his room and sat down with him and his detective-sergeant at the table he had once more moved out from against the wall.

'Except for Elaine,' said Johnny. 'But I've just seen her from the window skimming across the road.'

'Elaine's had the longest job of any of us,' said Peter. 'That is, if she got in everywhere. If she got in *anywhere*. She saw the porter at Stratton's block of flats, by the way. He was positive Innes had visited several times.'

Bob and Johnny were digesting this piece of hard news when Elaine burst in.

'Sorry to be late, Governor.' She was badly out of breath.

'You're not late, Elaine, we're early. Because we've done all we can for the time being. I gather you're straight off the job?'

232

'Yes, Governor.'

WPC Elaine Mitchell blushed, and her eyes slid away from Peter's. Aware of her propensity for cream cakes, he decided she'd stopped off to refuel, but only after her brief was completed.

'I was just telling the other members of the team about what you discovered this morning at Belmont Gardens.'

Elaine blushed again. 'The porter had no doubt about it, Governor. He only had to glance at the photo to be certain he'd seen Innes three or four times.'

'You didn't feel he was suppressing any feeling of suspicion, making any sort of connection in his mind between Innes and the current case?'

'Absolutely not,' Elaine assured him. 'In fact, it was after showing him the photograph that I suddenly knew he'd made up his mind to be on my side. And he didn't hesitate for a second about saying no when I asked him if he had any idea who my brother's contact in the building might be. It's awfully hard to look disappointed when you're wanting to sing with relief.'

'I can imagine,' said Peter. 'Well, WPC Mitchell, yours is the only piece of possible evidence I've heard so far against any of our three suspects. And if Geoff's and my experience is anything to go by, I'm hardly expecting to hear any other. Bob?'

'Don't be so bloody pessimistic, Peter. Johnny and I've got some possible evidence, too, and what's more it backs up Elaine's. We had a tremendous break last night, but we earned it. We followed Innes from his TV studios and watched him dithering about outside a tube station before deciding to catch a bus. It wasn't so easy keeping behind it and seeing when he got off – but we managed it. The bus decanted him outside a hostelry in the Fulham Road and we saw him go in. When we'd parked the car and got inside ourselves he was just ordering what we assumed was his second double whisky. No doubt even then that he was in a state, Governor. He was drinking with a purpose – to forget something. We each had a half at the counter and kept an eye on him. He alternated between staring into space and carrying on a dialogue with himself, and when he'd finished a third double he started looking round for his jacket. I shot off for the car – luckily we were between the day and the evening drinkers and we'd managed to park quite close – and had it at the front by the time Innes came out with Johnny just behind him. He was walking more slowly than he'd walked from the bus, and Johnny had to show his ID at one point to a uniformed man who, fair enough, was suspecting us of kerb-crawling. The second hostelry had a little car park round the back, and we went in there. We decided Innes was ripe for contact, which I made while Johnny stayed at the counter. Innes had another couple of doubles which I fetched for him, said a couple of rather weird things – about people being in cages – and then passed out. The landlord was delighted at the thought of losing him, and actually went through his pockets for us to find the address we could hardly admit to knowing already. He saw us off with great satisfaction, and we took Innes home. Two locks on the door, but we found his keys–' Bob Ryan glanced at Elaine, who shook her head, blushing again – 'and of course when we'd put him on his bed we took the opportunity of looking round. Nothing of any interest outside the bedroom apart from a photograph of the Gordon girl upside down at the bottom of a drawer–' Peter Hewitt tried to retain only one of his two reactions to this piece of information, the objective one – 'but in the bedroom, oh boy! Underneath the woollies in the bottom drawer – a stack of photographs.' Bob Ryan was unable to resist a dramatic pause. 'Every one of them of Charles Hugo Stratton.'

'The Super next stop on this one,' said Peter Hewitt into the stunned silence. 'But before we go on to that we'd better pool everything else, that's why I called this progress meeting. As we're on Innes, I'll begin with Geoff's and my experience of him.

Having just heard what we have from Elaine and Bob, I'll make a particular effort to be objective. But although he was sober when we saw him, there's no doubt he was nervous, his hands were trembling. And he admitted he'd been back on his own to see Stratton. But only once. To tell Stratton off for leading Annabel Gordon astray. Innes was way off beam there, Annabel Gordon wouldn't be so weakly suggestible. Unless, of course, she really was in love with Stratton… In view of those pics you turned up in Innes's drawer, Bob, I'm starting to see Innes's reactions in a different light.'

'He was wary of me, I can see now,' said Bob Ryan, 'because I was a man. Perhaps Stratton had introduced him to some ideas he hadn't got used to.'

'Innes looked surprised when I suggested he was jealous of Stratton,' continued Peter slowly, thinking as he went. 'Because the one he was jealous of was Annabel Gordon? By the time we spoke to him, at any rate, if not the first time he went to Stratton's flat.'

'He was breathing hard when he was telling us about that first visit to Stratton,' contributed Geoff. 'And there was a bit of colour in his face. Not a natural liar.'

'No.' Peter looked round at the absorbed faces before reluctantly going on. 'Samantha de Vere. Audrey Elsie Pinnington. Anything there? Geoff and I drew pretty

236

much of a blank, but Miss de Vere is a very self-controlled lady. Once or twice I had the impression she was thinking rather harder than her normal wont, but that's hardly evidence against her. She said she did sometimes have lunch with Stratton – well, we know that from his diary, and she'd know we know it – but that she hadn't been to his flat that day. She wasn't able to offer a real alibi, though – she said she'd lunched at the local crowded sandwich bar, which she did quite regularly. So we can't dismiss her. Geoff?

'Nothing to add,' said Geoff.

'Nor me,' said Elaine ruefully. 'I just meant to sit drinking tea and listening to her talking to her best friend... I did that, of course, and didn't get anything out of it, except to see how self-possessed Miss de Vere is, not to say smug at the contrast between herself and other less well-organized mortals, notably her friend Mandy... Anyway, she didn't give me any sort of an impression that she was unhappy, or worried, in fact that anything out of the way had happened anywhere near her. But I got up when her friend had gone and pretended to have an attack of cramp just by her table. She wasn't bothered whether I sat down there or not, and I made a fool of myself for absolutely nothing. Asking questions about her nail varnish and things like that,' said Elaine hastily, to Peter's raised eyebrows. 'That's all I mean. She told me where I could buy a bottle, and absolutely nothing else. Sorry.'

'You did well, Elaine,' soothed Peter automatically. 'And your experience dovetails with ours. Not much progress on Miss de Vere, then.' Peter paused again. 'Annabel Gordon. Bob?'

'Very nervous indeed,' said Bob Ryan promptly, and Johnny Boyle nodded. 'And unnervingly intelligent.'

'That was my experience. The intelligence.' Peter Hewitt tried to disregard his obtrusive sense of pleasure. 'What else, Bob?'

'I kept seeing the holes in our arguments while I was talking to her, something about her made them all seem as flimsy as they were. Then, at the end, I went through the form of reassurance again – reminding her that she wasn't the one who would go on trial, and so on – and it worked, she was suddenly a whole lot less nervous. Which means she wasn't in fact quite as bright as she seemed, or else really had been scared of us. Her alibi was even more unsatisfactory than Miss de Vere's: that she'd gone home alone at lunch-time that day, between photographic sessions. And like Miss de Vere, she admitted to having lunched chez Stratton from time to time, although not that particular day. She too, of course, could have made the admission because of knowing about the diary, or covering the possibility of it.'

'Of course.' Peter Hewitt looked round them again. 'I went after Annabel Gordon on my own. With Geoff at the end of the telephone. I felt–'

'The Governor felt he really ought to be able to manage by himself,' said Detective-Sergeant Hughes, grinning.

'A single man's less noticeable, and less memorable, than a pair.'

'Yes, you are a single man, aren't you, Peter?' commented Bob Ryan innocently.

'All right, yes, Annabel Gordon's an attractive woman.' Peter carried the war into the enemy's camp in the hope of getting it over. 'But if I'd tailed her to a political meeting, or even the cinema, I'd have rung for Sergeant Hughes. As it was, I followed her and escort into a disco. I asked her to dance while she was waiting to be brought a drink, and *my* break was that she noticed her partner being more interested in someone else. Which made her quite ready to accept my invitation to walk her home.'

'You went in?' asked Bob into the silence.

'I went in.' Peter steeled himself. 'For coffee, and the piece of information, when I commented on a large and prominent photograph of Stratton, that she and Stratton had been lovers. I asked her why she thought Mrs Trent had killed him and then called the police, and looking me candidly in the eye she said she had no idea. But she knew Stratton thought very highly of Mrs Trent. I had no feeling of any jealousy about that, she even said she'd liked Mrs Trent the one time she'd met her. When she gate-crashed the dinner party, that must have been.' Peter paused again. 'Then suddenly she burst into tears and said that in fact Stratton hadn't loved her, that when her ardour had started to exceed his he'd told her to take herself off.'

'It's not evidence,' murmured Bob Ryan. 'But it's impressive in its way.'

'So it's back to the Super?' asked Johnny Boyle. 'And not quite empty-handed?'

'That's it,' said Peter wearily. 'I'm pretty certain his next step then will be to authorize the questioning of Innes – we can't say how officially or unofficially, not knowing the situation with regard to the mysterious Mrs Trent – and if that draws a blank, I suppose the phase after that will be to go after relatives and friends and landladies and shop assistants. At which stage we'll wonder how we ever thought there was any slog in what we've been doing these last two days.' Beside him WPC Mitchell coughed. 'Oh, Elaine, forgive me. Did you manage to break and enter?'

'Two out of three,' said Elaine apologetically. 'And it didn't get me anywhere, I'm afraid. I didn't find a single thing which could possibly have a bearing on the mur-der–'

'Where did you draw blank?' interrupted Johnny Boyle. 'Innes's door would have been a toughie if the mortise–'

'–but gosh, I'd forgotten for a moment, I did find something. Something I – took away.' Elaine glanced warily at the Chief Inspector. 'Probably absurd, but I found an unlabelled cassette under some handker-chiefs in a top drawer, in a flat which didn't have a cassette-player. I took it really because it was – well, sort of illogical.'

Elaine's face now was begging for reassurance. 'Go on,' said Peter.

'I went to a shop nearby and bought a blank cassette and substituted it for the one I took. So that if the original was as signifi-cant as I just somehow felt it might be, it wouldn't be missed right away. I hope I did the right thing, Governor.' Elaine reached into her bag, found the cassette, and laid it on the table. 'It just made me think of the dog in the Sherlock Holmes story,' she explained diffidently. 'The one which didn't bark.'

CHAPTER 14

When she woke up the next morning, Samantha de Vere knew what she was going to do. In her mind as consciousness returned were the words with which her father had punctuated her childhood. *If you've got the advantage, girl, make use of it.*

Her father would have been referring to his daughter's looks, or her intelligence (funny to remember now, how promising she had been at maths), and usually annoying her into the bargain (sometimes, if he was facing the other way when he was speaking, she would mime the words as they came out, pulling a face), but the advice had stuck. In fact, now she thought about it, she had followed it so far in her life pretty consistently.

So why not this time?

Her decision made, Samantha got up from bed entirely calm and clear-headed. She did everything as usual, including going downstairs, after putting the kettle on, to buy a copy of her favourite tabloid news-paper from the stand outside the door of the building, and reading the first three pages of it over her toast and tea. Then washing up her few dishes and tidying round before going out to the pay telephone on the landing.

She rang Frank first.

'I'm so sorry, Frank, but I've woken with a migraine.' As there was never any animation in her voice, there was nothing she could do to act a blinding headache. But Frank had to be aware of how rarely his secretary/receptionist let him down.

'Oh dear, Samantha, how unpleasant for you.' Frank accorded Samantha's indisposition a ten-second silence. 'I *was* going to that hoteliers' lunch today, but if I can't get hold of Mrs Whitworth I can easily cancel–'

'Please don't do that, Frank, I was just going to say that if I lie down in the dark this morning I should be quite well enough by lunch-time to come in. No need to cancel your lunch party.'

'That's very thoughtful of you, Samantha. Very thoughtful indeed.' She could hear the relief in his voice. 'In that case I might not bother to contact Mrs Whitworth, if you really think that by lunch-time...'

'I'll be in by lunch-time.'

'I'll have to leave for the lunch by twelve-thirty.'

'I'll be in by twelve-thirty.'

'Thank you, Samantha. You go straight back to bed, now, and try to rest.'

'Thank you, Frank. I will.'

She already had Detective Chief Inspector

Hewitt's card propped up on the box in front of her, and she dialled the telephone number on it, then asked for the extension.

'CID.'

'Could I speak to Detective Chief Inspector Hewitt?' asked Samantha, reading out the main announcement on the card. 'This is Miss Samantha de Vere. Inspector Hewitt knows who I am.'

'Yes… Just a moment, please.'

She'd done it now, given her name, she had to go on, but she'd made the right decision, she still felt as calm as she'd felt when she first woke up, hearing those words of her dad's. *If you've got the advantage, girl, make use of it.*

Well, she had the advantage, all right.

'Detective Chief Inspector Hewitt here.' The voice sounded out of breath. 'Miss de Vere?' it inquired cautiously.

'Yes, Inspector, you asked me to get in touch with you if I – if I thought of anything else about Mrs Trent.'

'I did, Miss de Vere. Have you something else to tell me?'

'Yes, Inspector. Something I ought to have told you when you came to the hotel,' said Samantha humbly. 'I hadn't forgotten about it – well, it wasn't something anyone could forget about – but … well, it seemed like telling tales, somehow, and I just couldn't bring myself…'

'I think you'd better bring yourself round to Scotland Yard,' said Peter Hewitt gently, 'and tell me all about it.'

'Yes, all right,' responded Samantha, still outwardly meek but with a warm sense of triumph coursing through her body. 'Shall I come now?'

'It would be helpful if you could. Have you got a piece of paper so you can write down how to find me?'

Samantha wrote the Chief Inspector's instructions on the back of his card, then went to look at herself in her bathroom mirror, but her skin was so good – smooth and creamy-brown – and her hair so easy – needing only a brush or a comb down its shining length – there wasn't really anything special she could do to mark the importance of the occasion, beyond putting on her current favourite outfit – a white skirt and jacket.

She took a taxi to New Scotland Yard. If Detective Chief Inspector Hewitt was as impressed as the man on the desk downstairs, she could perhaps have a success in more than one direction.

When the lift doors opened, the Chief Inspector was waiting in person to receive her.

'Miss de Vere! Very good of you to come.'

She was, perhaps, surprised to find three other plain clothes policemen in the room

245

where the Chief Inspector led her, but not at all dismayed. They sat her down in the midst of them.

'Now, Miss de Vere,' began the Chief Inspector – he was obviously the most senior one – as soon as they'd made sure she was comfortable. 'What is it you have to tell us?'

'It's about – Mrs Trent,' said Samantha, all at once a bit nervous. 'You see – I didn't tell you the truth when you came to the hotel, I did go and see Mr Stratton – that day. We – we hadn't made a lunch date or anything, but we spoke on the telephone during the morning and he suggested I pop round, so of course I did. I was – very fond of Mr Stratton.' She didn't have to force the tears to the surface, all at once they were there. 'When I got to his front door I was just going to ring the bell when I saw the door wasn't quite closed. I pushed it open, and right away I heard voices. They were loud, angry... I recognized Mr Stratton, but not the woman at first. I – I'm afraid I closed the front door behind me, Inspector, and then tiptoed across the hall.' Samantha directed the full force of her wide-eyed gaze on to the Chief Inspector, then distributed the waning beam among his junior officers. 'I got almost to the sitting-room door, Mr Stratton and Mrs Trent were so – so busy quarrelling they didn't see me. Anyway, they were sort of sideways on to me, looking at

246

each other all the time. Mrs Trent was standing with her back to the cupboard where Mr Stratton keeps – kept – his gun.'

'You knew about the gun?' interrupted the fattest of the four men.

'Everybody knew about it. Mr Stratton used to take it out and say he was bored and was going to play his favourite game. Russian ... Russian rollette...'

'Russian roulette, yes,' said Peter Hewitt. 'Did you ever see him fire the gun, Miss de Vere?'

'No, and I never thought he would. It was just...'

'Just a gesture?' supplied Peter. 'I understand, yes. But this time?'

'It was Mrs Trent who took the gun out this time,' said Samantha, being careful not to speak too eagerly. 'She pointed it at him, and he said, "Don't, Olga," or something like that, and then–'

'Miss de Vere,' interrupted the Chief Inspector gently. 'This is such important evidence, obviously we shall want you to come with us to Mr Stratton's flat so that you can show us precisely what happened. So I think the most helpful thing would be if we all went along there now, to save you having to tell your story all the way through twice. And then a third time when you give us your statement. If we do it this way, you'll only have to go through it a couple of times.'

He was smiling at her reassuringly, but all at once Samantha felt wary, uncertain. It had never crossed her mind that telling the police about Hugo and Mrs Trent would involve her in going back to Hugo's flat. She ought to have realized it, though of course things weren't really taking a turn which need worry her – now she thought about it, it was inevitable they would want her on the spot, such a vital witness...

'Of course, Inspector.'

She sat in the back of the car between the Chief Inspector and one of the detective-sergeants. The other two policemen were in the front.

'Did you speak to the porter when you went into Belmont Gardens – that day?' the Chief Inspector asked her as they drove comfortably along. Really, they were making her feel quite VIP.

'He wasn't there,' said Samantha. 'It was just after a quarter to one, and he goes for his lunch about then. There's another man who comes on while he's out, Mr Stratton said once that they're supposed to overlap but sometimes they don't.'

'So no one was there that day, Miss de Vere, no one saw you go in?'

'No. I don't think so anyway, Inspector,' said Samantha, thoroughly relaxed again despite the slight but disagreeable smell of sweat near at hand. She didn't think it was the Chief Inspector.

'Thank you, Miss de Vere. And what about your departure? I gather – now I'm not passing judgement, it must have been a terrifying experience for you – I gather you crept away as unnoticed as you crept in?'

'Well – yes. I–'

'Did you leave the building the same way you came in?'

She had jerked on the seat, the two men had probably been aware of it. They probably asked questions specially when driving with suspects, so that they could feel their reactions in the upholstery. Thank goodness she was only a vital witness.

'No, I didn't, Inspector. I'm afraid – I went down the fire escape at the end of the corridor. There's a door there you can open from the inside, and then just walk down. Hugo – Mr Stratton – showed it to me once when he was in one of his jokey moods, telling me how you could make a quick getaway. I know it was wrong, Inspector, that's why I rang you up this morning, but at the time… Well, I just didn't want to have any connection with what I'd seen. And Mr Stratton was dead when I ran out, I couldn't have done anything for him.' The tears were there again, and surreptitiously she smeared them down her cheeks.

'I see, Miss de Vere. Yes, of course. All entirely understandable. So you didn't see anyone when you left the building? Either on Mr Stratton's floor, or on the way down the fire escape, or when you reached the ground?'

'No one, no. I was terribly relieved at the time. But now...'

'Thank you, Miss de Vere. We appreciate that you've come to us.'

'Well...' She bridled modestly.

'Better late than never!' said the detective in the front passenger seat, turning round. Samantha hadn't been sure whether or not the men in the front of the car could hear them.

'That's what I thought...'

'It must have taken some courage, Miss de Vere. More courage the longer you left it.'

There was no doubt the Chief Inspector was looking at her admiringly.

'It did,' she said simply. 'But I feel better now.'

They didn't talk again, then, until the car had drawn up right outside the doors of Belmont Gardens.

'Here we are!' said the driver, and the detective-sergeant beside her leapt instantly out and leaned in again to assist her. He was definitely the one with the B.O. 'Ever watch detective series on TV, Miss de Vere?' he asked her as he walked beside her into the building.

'I'm afraid I haven't really done, no, but I

shall now,' she responded graciously. She would, too, she would have quite a different attitude to series about the police. Really, it was quite exciting, travelling about with these four important men. And it helped take her mind off Hugo. If only she wasn't having to go back to the flat. As the lift took them up she was more and more aware of her heartbeat.

It was all very tidy, and there were no evidences whatsoever of Hugo's presence. Nor of his final moments, which was a relief. Nevertheless she hung back in the hall.

'That's right, Miss de Vere,' said the Chief Inspector encouragingly. 'It'll help us if you'll stand where you were standing when you watched Mr Stratton quarrelling with Mrs Trent, and tell us just what you saw and heard. Have you found the spot?'

'This is it.'

The Chief Inspector and one of the younger detectives had gone ahead of her into the sitting-room, while the other two had disappeared – they could be in a bedroom, or the kitchen, or still at the front door behind her, she couldn't hear them and somehow now that she had decided on the spot she felt unable to turn round.

'Now, Miss de Vere,' said the Chief Inspector, 'perhaps if Detective-Sergeant Hughes and I take the parts of Mr Stratton and Mrs Trent? I'm sorry if this is distressing for you, but you'll have realized the sort of thing which would be necessary when you were brave enough to telephone me...'

'That's quite all right, Chief Inspector.' She hadn't called him Chief Inspector before, and this, she now realized, had been remiss of her.

'Was it like this?' asked Peter Hewitt. He was standing with his back to the drawer where Hugo had kept his gun, his detective-sergeant was standing opposite. So the Chief Inspector was going to play the part of – of Mrs Trent. Well, it was the main part.

'That's exactly right, Chief Inspector.'

'Good. Now, Miss de Vere, if you could tell us what happened, and we'll try to act it out. All right?'

'Yes, that's all right.' It wasn't, though. All at once she was feeling physically sick, seeing Hugo on the floor again even though all she was actually looking at was two men standing facing one another. She made an effort. 'When I'd got – here – and was able to see and hear them properly, neither of them was speaking. Mrs Trent was reaching behind her into that drawer, and bringing the gun out. She pointed it at Mr Stratton still without saying anything, and he took a step back and said "Don't be a fool," or something like that...' The awfulness of the memory was threatening to confuse her, but she clung savagely to her self-control.

252

'Actually, Chief Inspector, he said "Don't be a fool, Olga." Then – then she seemed to take hold of the gun more firmly, point it more, and – and I heard a click. I suppose it must have been the safety-catch. Mr Stratton said "For God's sake–" I'm sure that's right – and then Mrs Trent said "Nobody says that to me–" or something like that – and then – then she just pulled the trigger and – and – Hugo fell backwards on to the floor.' She knew she might do the same if she didn't quickly lean against something. Luckily she was near enough to the bookcase in the hall to use it discreetly. It was just as well that the strain of getting her story across was absorbing all her energies, saving her from really feeling the fact that she was talking about the killing of Hugo.

'And then you left, Miss de Vere?'

'Well – yes, Chief Inspector. I mean, I was suddenly terrified that now she was – on her own – Mrs Trent might look round. The gun had made quite a noise and she must have been afraid someone had heard it. And she could have remembered that the front door wasn't quite shut.' Samantha now felt strong enough to leave the support of the bookcase and advance through the doorway into the sitting-room. Relief and confidence were returning with each steadying heartbeat. 'So – well, I turned and went out of the flat as quickly and as quietly as I could. It felt like ages while I was fiddling with the fire escape door, she'd only have had to come to the door of Mr Stratton's flat to see me…' In her mind's eye she was watching herself tearing frantically at the catch.

'You left, then, Miss de Vere, before you saw what Mrs Trent did in fact do next?'

'That's right, Chief Inspector. Might I sit down, now?' she asked, very slightly plaintive.

'Of course, Miss de Vere, forgive us… All right? Good. So you didn't see Mrs Trent recoil from what she'd done? You didn't see her fall back against the table – there – carrying the cassette-recorder?'

'No.' She hadn't so much as glanced at that table, or what was on it, the whole of the time she'd been looking into Hugo's sitting-room, but now that the Chief Inspector had mentioned it, she all at once couldn't keep her eyes off it. 'No, but I don't see what–'

'When Mrs Trent bumped against that table it reminded her about the cassette-recorder on it. There was a cassette in the recorder, in the act of recording. Whether Mrs Trent knew this already, and now remembered it, or whether she just saw the cassette and took it in case it might have been incriminating her, we don't know. We do know, though, that Mrs Trent didn't have a cassette-recorder of her own, so it's quite likely she wouldn't have known whether or not the cassette was in process of recording, or how to erase it if it was, and she might well have taken it just to be on the safe side. Anyway, she took it away with her.'

The Chief Inspector, and his voice, had suddenly gone very faint and far away, and the room had become a funny shape. Samantha was surprised to hear her own voice sounding normal.

'But Mrs Trent didn't go away, Chief Inspector. She stayed here and telephoned the police.'

'Of course she did, Miss de Vere. How silly of me. I must have started to take my cue from you, saying Mrs Trent when I meant Audrey Elsie Pinnington.' Three of them were suddenly standing round the chair where she was sitting. 'Audrey Elsie Pinnington,' repeated the Chief Inspector, across the now vast gulf which separated her from the rest of the world, 'you are not obliged to say anything unless you wish to do so, but whatever you say will be taken down in writing and may be given in evidence...'

'Here it is,' said another voice, and there was a short silence, and then Hugo said, 'All right, Sam, as you're here you can have it now.'

She thought she had screamed, but no one seemed to have noticed, so it must have happened inside her. She tried to tell them to stop it, not to let her hear any more, but she couldn't speak.

'Hugo…'

She was speaking then. But only just.

'Look, Sam, we've had some fun right? But it's over. O-V-E-R. Frankly, my dear, you bore me to death.'

So that's what she did.

She couldn't speak, but she could laugh. When she had laughed for a long, long time, one of the detectives tapped her sharply on the cheek and she stopped laughing.

'Sam? What are you doing? Sam… Don't be a fool, Sam. No, Sam, no!'

'Nobody says that to *me*.'

'For God's sake, Sam… Sam!'

There was a muffled explosion. It reminded her of the gas fire in her bedsitter, and it blasted her free of the paralysis. She sprang to her feet.

'You shouldn't have said that, Hugo!' she shouted. 'You shouldn't have said that to *me!* You didn't mean it, you couldn't have meant it, but I couldn't let you say it again, and I couldn't let you send me away. You couldn't go on living, Hugo, and not be with *me*…' There was a woman helping the four men to get her sitting down again, but when she was in the chair she suddenly went limp and began to cry. 'If I'd gone for his head,' she sobbed, 'I'd have been more sure of killing him. But I couldn't spoil his beautiful face.'

Part Three

CHAPTER 15

At the third and last meeting of the elite sub-committee, which took place in Peter Hewitt's office the moment Peter and his sergeant had handed Miss Pinnington over to the Chief Superintendent and a couple of strange men, the mood was thoughtful and subdued.

'If I'd played Elaine's cassette in the office last night,' said Peter ruefully, 'instead of taking it home and forgetting it until this morning because of being obsessed with thoughts of Innes, we'd have got to Miss de Vere before she got to us and no doubt have spared ourselves that charade. I'm sorry, Elaine, I didn't take you seriously enough.'

'That's all right, Governor,' said Elaine, while the others were respectfully silent. But Peter knew how lucky he'd been that his less than total conscientiousness hadn't queered their investigation.

'It's silly,' pursued Elaine, 'but I keep feeling the cassette was a cheat. A sort of short cut which saved us doing all the real work of getting Samantha de Vere to confess.'

'I know what Elaine means,' said Peter. 'It was suddenly too easy. In any case, though, Miss de Vere was on the way to condemning herself out of her own mouth. She just couldn't leave well alone. She didn't have the limited but vital piece of information about Mrs Trent which *we* are privileged to possess, and which meant we also knew that the probably accurate scene she described between Stratton and Mrs Trent must have had a different protagonist. And if she was there that lunch-time – then she was the one. As simple as that.'

'Only we'd still be trying to prove it,' said Bob Ryan.

'Yes, yes, I know. This is just luxury talk. Now – our special duties are satisfactorily discharged and it only remains for me to dissolve our *ad hoc* committee. After I've thanked you all for your splendid support.' He turned to Elaine. 'And expressed our particular gratitude to WPC Mitchell for her brilliant decision to remove that cassette. And replace it. I'm not sticking my neck out, Elaine, when I say that I'm quite sure you'll be in line for a commendation. And possibly promotion.'

'Thank you, Governor. Over-confidence played it's part, didn't it? I mean, if Samantha de Vere – Audrey Pinnington – hadn't been so sure the powers that be believed Mrs Trent was the killer, and that therefore she was in the clear, she'd have destroyed that cassette, wouldn't she?'

'I'm certain she would. And something else has struck me. Stratton, on the form he's shown to date, might just have set the cassette up in order to record his dismissal of Samantha de Vere for enjoyment again later. If he did, he paid for his spot of sadism.' Peter looked round the table, aware that WPC Mitchell was shuddering. 'Thank you all again for your invaluable assistance. Everything will be in my report.'

'Thanks, Governor.'

Each one of them, he noticed, got up reluctantly. They'd been a team for less than three days but it felt like a lot longer and those few days would redound favourably for them all, probably for years to come...

As the sound of the last pair of shoes receded along the corridor, Peter turned to his telephone. Research on the number he wanted had been carried out already, officially.

'Would it be possible to speak to Annabel Gordon? Peter Hewitt here.'

Miraculously they found her, but it was that kind of day.

'Hello. May I see you again? Tonight, for instance?'

There was a fractional pause, in which his life passed in review.

'Yes!' she said at last, cheerfully. 'I should

like that.'

'Good. Shall I pick you up at work? At home?'

'Come to the flat. Seven?'

'Fine. Goodbye, now.'

'Goodbye.'

He'd have a lot of explaining to do, reflected Peter as he left his office, and he didn't know yet how long or how full his story could be. Or, of course, whether once he had embarked on it he would be allowed to stay with her long enough to bring it to an end. Or whether he would tell her anything about Stratton...

'Once upon a time there was a policeman who had to go and see a woman officially, and when his superiors lost interest in her and he was able to go and see her unofficially, he was very happy...'

He might begin like that.

Or he might postpone his explanation to another time. The main thing was that he was going to see her again.

CHAPTER 16

When Henry first went into the tiny room where Olga was at least on her own he thought she was asleep, she was lying so still. But as he drew the chair over to the bed, lifting it clear of the rough floor so that it wouldn't disturb her, he saw that her eyes were open, staring unblinkingly at the low grey ceiling.

'Olga?' It was only a week, but her nose was sharper in profile, her cheekbones even more prominent, and the harsh overhead light showed her hair to be a dark dusty colour rather than the rich brown he still imagined it.

'Henry.'

She turned her head on the pillow so that she was looking at him, and brought her hand up from under the blanket for him to take hold of. There was no expression in her eyes.

'Olga,' he said again. 'They've found Hugo's murderer. But it's all right, darling, I've something else to tell you...' Her eyes were still blank as he stared into them, but slowly they filled with the very essence of fear. At the same time her body started to tremble, and the hand he was holding began an almost rhythmic clutching and letting go. 'Oh no. Olga!'

He had done it the wrong way. Perhaps disastrously, agonized Henry, as he tried and failed to gain response from his wife's frantic face. He should have begun with the revelation which would have ended her ordeal on the instant, and only then told her she was free.

'I won't leave here, Henry, I won't! No one can make me!'

'You'll go to the hospital,' said Henry, trying to smooth the cold damp forehead which slipped away from under his hand as Olga wrenched backwards and forwards on the pillow. 'The prison hospital, I mean. I promise you, you won't have to leave this building until you tell me you're ready.'

She didn't seem to hear him, and there didn't seem to be any point in trying to tell her the rest. Perhaps the way he'd played it, he'd sent her over the edge.

Henry got to his feet and went the few steps to the door, which was ajar.

'Afraid I've made a mess of things,' he said miserably to the two men waiting beyond it, mandatorily out of earshot. 'She's – not well.'

The doctor was there very quickly, and gave Olga an injection. He told Henry he was taking her into the hospital, and that he could come back the next morning and try to talk to her again.

'Not until then?'

'There'd be no point, Mr Trent, she's in deep shock.'

'I see... If she asks for me, though...'

'I don't think she will but we'll let you know.'

The doctor wore that half-puzzled, half-questioning look which tended to appear on prison faces whenever Olga was the subject at issue... He'd need to do some telephoning as soon as he got away, explain why they'd have to wait a bit longer (he wouldn't tell them the reason might be at his own door, it wouldn't do any good and he didn't want to put it into words). And be in good time to collect the children... No, it was all right, Pam was collecting them today and taking them back with her until he went for them... 'At whatever time,' Pam had told him cheerfully. 'Don't worry, Henry.'

He had become an expert at avoiding people he knew on the train, but tonight he was so preoccupied he let Jack Shepherd from three doors down slip past his guard.

'How's Olga, Henry?' Jack was the more embarrassed of the two of them, finding himself at the other end of Henry's abstracted gaze, but at least he wasn't pretending, as some of them did, that Henry had all at once become a single man.

'Not too good,' said Henry.

'When – when's the trial?'

'Early December.' If there had been going to be a trial, it would have been somewhere about then.

'If there's anything Edna and I can do...'

'Thanks, Jack. That's good of you.'

'How's Mummy?' was the chorus on Pam's step. It had been a choice between keeping the children away from school and pretending Olga was in hospital, or letting them carry on with their normal lives after telling them before anyone else did that she was in prison because she had told the police she had killed Uncle Hugo. Henry had explained to them that of course Mummy hadn't done what she had said she had. She had found Uncle Hugo's dead body and confessed to killing him because she wasn't well, and soon everyone would know the truth. Meanwhile, Martin had had a playground fight, and come off the victor. Henry couldn't let himself think what the situation might be doing to the pair of them.

'She sends her love.' He kissed the children and Pam, then took Lucy into his arms. 'She's not feeling too good today,' he murmured over Lucy's head.

'Oh, Henry.' Pam's round bright face clouded.

'But the doctor's sedated her and I think she'll be better tomorrow. I also think the time has come when it would do her good to see you, Pam. I'm sorry it's been so long.'

'Do you really?' The expressive face was radiant. 'That would be wonderful, I've missed her so much.'

'If you can manage just to talk about the sort of things I imagine you talk about over your morning coffees at the kitchen table…'

'Of course! Don't worry, Henry, I won't upset her. When can I go?' Pam held out her arms as Lucy, having mauled her father about to her temporary satisfaction, showed signs of transferring her attentions.

'Could you manage tomorrow afternoon? Or the next one, if you're working–'

'I'm not working, tomorrow afternoon would be marvellous. What time?'

'Three o'clock seems to be a good time. She's in the hospital block, which is really why I think she's going to feel better. More light and air.'

'Oh, Henry… Of course, I'll go at three.'

'Good.' He hesitated. 'Are you working the day after tomorrow?'

'Only in the morning.'

'Well, keep three o'clock that day on ice, Pam, in case Olga isn't well enough tomorrow. But if you haven't heard from me by lunch-time, take it she's expecting you.'

'That's fine, Henry.'

He didn't sleep well, dissatisfied with himself and listening for the telephone even though he knew it wouldn't ring. After breakfast he drove the children to school, then went straight on to the prison.

'She's awake,' the doctor told him in the small office at the entrance to the hospital block. 'Not responsive, but she washed herself, and drank a cup of tea.'

'Thanks. And thanks for looking after her.'

Olga was lying as she had been lying the day before, only in a better bed with superior bedclothes and more space around her.

'Darling,' said Henry, taking her hand and refusing to be deterred by the restored blankness of her eyes, 'will you listen to me while I talk a bit?'

Her hand didn't respond and she didn't speak or move her head.

'I'll talk anyway,' he said. 'And just hope you can hear me.' He had official clearance, but he was still aware of the strength of a working lifetime's discipline of absolute discretion, of hiding his trade secret unless and until there was no alternative to revealing it. Well, there was no alternative now. 'Olga, I know why you pretended to have killed Hugo, I know it was because you wanted to go to prison so that they couldn't get at you any more, so that the children would be safe.'

Somewhere during his clumsy sentence her hand had come to life, even though it had gone limp again. He was enormously encouraged.

'I know, darling, because I'm trained to know that sort of thing. Olga, when you met me I was a civil engineer, and that's what I've been ever since. But when you met me I was working for British Intelligence, and I've been doing that ever since, too. Olga?'

He heard the heavy sigh, and was aware of the abrupt relaxation of her body. She still didn't speak, or look at him, but her fingers arched briefly against his hand.

'When – they – let you leave the USSR, I was afraid it must be at a price. I know them. And – one day there was a tension in you, suddenly you weren't always meeting my eyes... Once or twice in your sleep... Especially after those fantastic weeks in town were over, when we'd got into the house. At least, I felt, I was with you, I could look out for the signs – in the future – which would show me I was right. You didn't know it, but you had just about the best antidote for your trouble absolutely at hand... After a while I began to forget about it for days, weeks, at a time. I expect you did, too...' Henry paused, hopeful, and received another faint acknowledgement of the hand. 'In a way I was frightened when we had Martin, I suspected they'd been waiting for him. But nothing happened, not even when Lucy arrived. I really began to relax. And then – you changed, darling. In the course of one day.'

Still holding her hand he leaned back against the uncomfortable slats of his chair, waiting. She didn't move her head, but eventually she began very quietly to speak.

'They telephoned. In the morning. They reminded me I had two young children. I thought – they'll make me get another job, get established, then start stealing secrets. It was bad enough thinking *that*. Underneath, of course, I was thinking they must know how good a shot I'd been. Remembering that time in the park... But I couldn't face that – until they made me. Henry, I had to go somewhere – I don't know where – and practise shooting at targets with circles on their heads and hearts. I don't know how I went on living.' She ignored his oath. 'Well, I just about decided not to–'

'Oh, my darling!'

'Are you surprised?' she asked angrily, jerking bolt upright and turning to glare at him. 'You? With that special knowledge you're telling me now that you've had all this time?'

'No, I'm not surprised. And Olga, within a day of the change in you, I'd started using that knowledge.'

'But not to reassure *me!* Until five minutes ago, Henry, I was still seeing suicide as the only alternative to being safe in prison.'

He bowed his head. 'I knew, I knew!' he murmured wretchedly.

'But you couldn't risk your precious cover!'

'I hadn't got clearance,' he flashed back. 'Do you think I would have held back for any other reason? The rules can't be broken for anyone, Olga, not even for you!'

'Oh, Henry!'

Able to weep at last, she flung herself into his arms. She knew it was the best moment of her life, even though she was still too crushed and weak to be able to savour it. Too well adapted to the burden to be able properly to realize it had been lifted.

'I thought – I thought last night that I really had sent you over the edge,' Henry was murmuring. 'Forgive me, darling, I should have said what I've just said now before telling you you'd lost your claim to be Hugo's killer.'

'Something happened last night when you told me they'd found the murderer. When I realized I'd lost my hiding place I saw madness for a moment. And when I woke up this morning – it was a special sort of sleep, wasn't it? – I decided it was a good idea, to be mad. The only idea, apart from suicide, and I could always come back to that.' She felt him shudder in her arms. 'And I *was* – am – really too feeble at the moment to have proper reactions to things. Well, that's how I felt when you came in.' She found herself drawing a little away from

Henry in order to smile at him, the first unmanufactured smile she had managed for what seemed a very long time.

'I suppose it was that dumb blonde who killed Hugo,' she said, when they had released one another except for their hands. 'The one who was there for dinner that night. Samantha, wasn't it? I've been thinking about it since I found – Hugo's body – and that was the solution I kept coming back to. She was jealous of me even for pouring out coffee.'

His astonished stare had her smiling again, before she realized it.

'Yes, it was. The police should have come to you instead of bothering to set up a very difficult unofficial official investigation. It could equally well have been one of the pair who gatecrashed.'

'I suppose so, but somehow I never really thought of either of them as a possibility. They were so embarrassingly human. Samantha was hardly human at all.'

'Simple, isn't it?' he responded, grinning.

'She wasn't the type to give herself up, Henry.'

'She didn't. As I said, the police mounted an unofficial investigation.'

'At the suggestion of you and your organization?'

'Well, yes.'

Suddenly there was one thing – a new

thing – more important than anything else. 'Tell me honestly, darling. Did you think – at first – that I could have killed Hugo?'

Although he didn't rush into a passionate denial, at least he was looking her in the eyes. 'Not for the reason you gave. Never that, Olga. Otherwise, at first, I didn't know what to think. You see, I remembered your skills with firearms, and your successful encounter with the Moscow mugger, and my first thought had to be that Hugo was the target you'd been set, obviously on a reminder about Martin and Lucy. But at the same time I couldn't abandon my belief that even under provocation such as that you would be incapable of taking life. I mean, you can't even kill a fly, my darling.' Henry paused to kiss her. 'Hugo was always being mysterious about himself, and it seemed entirely in character that he might belong to some undercover group, even though I'd never encountered him myself. So the first thing, seeing that you'd successfully taken care of your own and the children's security, was to set up an investigation of Hugo. From my – privileged position – I was able to mobilize a team, and it was obvious within days that Hugo didn't have my kind of other life. Oh darling, when I realized that all you had done was to happen on someone else's *crime passionel...*'

'You should have realized it at once.' But

she spoke lazily, recovering to awareness that the future was no longer unthinkable.

'In my guts I did… We used to joke about Hugo having it coming to him, didn't we? There was no psychological difficulty in believing Hugo had been killed by a jealous man or woman.'

'Man, Henry?'

'Yes, darling. You didn't see for yourself, and I knew Hugo was glad you didn't… Hugo was only intermittently prepared to make love to women and I don't think he would ever have married, put himself in the position of having to be always sexually available to one. He liked women if they were intelligent, and in that case he liked them too much to associate them with the behaviour which didn't come to him as naturally as he would have liked. That, I think, is why he never came out of the closet – he *wanted* to be a normal full-blooded heterosexual like me.' They grinned at one another. 'He had a heart to heart talk with me once. His mother had been very anxious for him to "find a nice girl and settle down", and he'd been so devoted to her he really had tried. The paradox is that it could have been that very devotion which made it impossible for him.'

'Hence the Samanthas… I'll have to get used to it … that was why you were so certain Hugo wasn't in love with me, when I was a bit afraid that he might be.'

'Yes.'

'And so certain he wouldn't have assaulted me,' she said sadly. Then shivered. 'Henry, if what you've just told me about Hugo had come out, I wouldn't have had a defence.'

'Perhaps not. Don't think of it.'

'He liked me better than any other woman, I always knew that. And I've been the one to destroy his reputation in such a disgusting way, telling the world he tried to ... Hugo!' Now she was free of the nightmare – whatever was to be done now would be done with Henry – she was free to contemplate her appalling betrayal.

'We'll see,' said Henry. Somewhere the far side of her weakness and weariness she saw this as a rather strange response. 'When I discovered there was no reason for you to have killed Hugo, I realized you must have decided to take advantage of finding him dead to secure yourself asylum. Thank God, then, I was in a position to be able to persuade my bosses to let the top echelons of the police in on the situation and get them to set up a murder investigation. Samantha's on ice, by the way, until we're all safely out of the way. So far as the public's concerned you're still under arrest for Hugo's murder. And that's how it will be until you and Martin and Lucy and I have disappeared... What is it, darling?'

Her face must have resumed reflecting her

reactions. 'The children, Henry! I must really have been ill last night, I'd forgotten... That terrible worry I had before – before I was brought here, that's gone now, they can't get at me through the children – at the moment.' Her heart proved it could still contract when she thought of the children, even now she had Henry. 'But ... life must be impossible for them. Their friends won't treat them normally any more and they'll have to listen to things being said about me...'

'Don't worry about the children, Olga, they're safe at school and I'll be there to meet them when they come out and this time I'll be bringing them here.'

Her mind caught up with something he had said.

'Disappeared... How can we disappear?'

'By courtesy of the Establishment.' He paused, his eyes warning her he was about to say something she wouldn't want to hear. 'Exile, Olga. We've got to get lost.'

'But, Henry... Why should *you*... Oh, darling, your work, the firm, the garden...'

To her amazement she saw tears running down his cheeks. 'That's your reaction, is it, Olga, anxiety about *me?* Oh, darling...' Henry blew his nose. 'I couldn't live without you, even if they let me and they might not – and the children will certainly have to vanish. So really, there's no alternative for any of us.'

'It would have seemed terrible a few weeks

ago,' she murmured, leaning up to touch his wet face. 'Now it seems dazzling. If it can be managed.' Always that terrible fear, waiting to pounce back.

'It can. Would you like some more tea?'

'Yes.' She lay back, watching Henry's precious self cross the room and go out of the door. She didn't think she would ever really relax again unless she was in sight of him. He came back very quickly and sat by her in silence, playing with her hair, until the tray of tea and biscuits was brought in by a nurse.

'One thing my subconscious persists in wanting to know,' he said, the moment the nurse was out of the room. 'Why did you go and see Hugo that day?'

'Oh, Henry! I went to ask his advice about what I should do. Hugo was so devastatingly practical at times – because of his own strong instinct for self-preservation, I suppose – the thought of pouring it all out to him was like – like the last thin veil hanging between me and suicide. I knew, of course, that even if they hadn't been listening to me telephoning Hugo they'd be watching me, and I made a point of carrying that ridiculous book he lent you at the end of that dinner party. There was no one on the porter's desk, and I'm sure no one – apart from them – saw me go in. I found Hugo's front door open, and then – Hugo. I was going to rush away when I suddenly realized Hugo had helped me after all.'

'If you'd only confided in *me*, darling.'

'I don't know how I managed not to. I suppose I always remembered just in time that the house was bound to be bugged, and if we went driving off somewhere... Even if I told you in a restaurant, say, under cover of some pop music, I felt we'd somehow give ourselves away.'

'Yes, I can see–'

'I love you so much, Henry, I don't mind where we go, or how far away.'

'Neither do I, so long as we're all together.' He strained her against him. 'It will be soon, darling. Olga, what is it?'

Suddenly limp, she had fallen back on to the pillow.

'I've just remembered – where have I *been*, Henry? – the man I was supposed to kill...'

'Good God, Olga, it had got to that? When we found Hugo was in the clear we thought you must still be waiting.'

'Oh no.' The anxiety she should have felt days ago for her intended victim had seized her by the throat and she could barely whisper. 'Henry, you'd better warn him. There won't be any difficulty, I know his name and where he lives. A man called Ian Bartholomew. I thought I'd seen his name in the paper–'

'Ian Bartholomew!' Henry shouted the

name, and an obscenity, and leapt to his feet. 'Telephone! I must find a telephone! Dear God, not Ian!' He ran out of the room.

'So you know him,' she said, when ten minutes later he was back with her and taking her hand. Anxiety had turned to dread. 'Is he all right?'

'Thank God, yes. Evidently the KGB haven't got their act together since you let them down. Which is a piece of luck, Ian does tend to be a thorn in Red flesh... Olga, Ian Bartholomew's at the top of the Intelligence tree as well as a good friend of mine. It was he who got the police to lay on the murder inquiry when I told him ... when I told him the true story.' She was aware of his eyes sliding away from her, but all her attention was on her self-disgust for her negligence.

'I should have got a message to him. But I didn't remember... There's another thing, Henry. They sent me the key to a locker at Paddington which has the gun in it I was supposed to use. The same way they sent me another locker key before that, so that I could collect my instructions. I hid the second key at the back of my bottom drawer, wrapped up with some notes I'd made.'

'I looked for clues,' said Henry, trying to smile. 'But when I got to that particular drawer and found a plastic bag with a lethal dose of drugs I didn't look any further. We'll

277

have the gun collected today. Unless someone got in and found the key... Olga, the four of us must softly and silently vanish away. And secretly. No goodbyes. Which reminds me, I told Pam last night you'd see her this afternoon if you felt well enough. Tomorrow afternoon, if not.' Henry paused, gazing at her, and Olga thought she read his message. *Please let it be this afternoon, because tonight I would prefer you to be unavailable.* 'I'm insulting you by putting it into words, but I must. No indication even to Pam that you aren't still under arrest. That I'm anything but the old familiar fuddy-duddy Henry. You can even say you think the trial will be sometime in December. In this business there can be no exceptions.'

'I know that, don't I?'

'Oh, darling, forgive me.' Henry paused, and Olga thought he went on with an effort. 'If of course you feel it would be too painful to see Pam at all and you'd rather not...'

'It will be painful, but if I have the chance of seeing Pam again, I want to take it. And I'm quite well enough today.'

'Good. I suggested three o'clock.' Henry got up again, the movement she had been dreading. 'I must go, darling. Almost for the last time.'

'I know. When will you be back?'

'Late afternoon. Five o'clock.'

'With the children, you said.'

'Yes.' Again his eyes slid away from hers. 'When I collect them from school today I'll bring them to you here.'

CHAPTER 17

Her instinct was to pack, although she didn't seem to have anything beyond a dressing-gown, a pair of slippers, and the contents of a sponge bag, and nothing to put them into. Anyway, if she was to obey Henry to the letter, not even Pam must be allowed to see evidences of a departure which could indicate no more than a transfer from a hospital cell to a cell in the main prison.

Which she would probably have been well enough to go back to, she was in touch again. And regretful, almost dismayed, that sleep, the ally which since she had been locked up had allowed her such generous respite from her thoughts and her fears, had suddenly retreated.

She couldn't even relax, and paced about the small room, excited, she supposed, by the prospect of a future which at least was imaginable. And agonizing, now that the end of agony was so near, to have Martin and Lucy safe beside her.

Henry will see to it.

That was the answer to every anxiety surging to the surface of Olga's mind. Not the sort of answer she had once automatically accorded the anxieties thrown up by her daily life, but it would be a long time before she could face that on her own again – before she would be capable of it, and before circumstances would give her back a freedom of choice. If they ever did. Just now, that seemed the least thing to concern her.

By the time her lunch came in, bodily exhaustion had taken her back to bed. She didn't want to eat the ample portion of cottage pie and carrots, but forced it down with vague thoughts of keeping her strength up. Or restoring it. Moving her hands over her body, Olga realized she had lost weight. Would she get it back in the sunshine, or in heated rooms?

Henry will decide.

Or his bosses. The men who had been able to discover, in a matter of days, that Hugo the mysterious was no more than a good photographer. While that nice, unexciting chap Henry Trent... Who did, though, look incredibly like everybody's mental picture of Lord Peter Wimsey... And it was Henry who had solved the only real mystery about Hugo, the mystery of the Samanthas. And she who... But when she and Henry and Martin and Lucy disappeared, the world would know it was Samantha who had killed Hugo, and then they would know that he hadn't assaulted Olga Trent. To make sure everyone knew, she might even write a disclaimer and have it sent to a newspaper.

Henry would see to it.

If only she had known that Henry would see to things, she would have been spared the ten years in which fear had lived in the corner of her mind like a waiting beast. It had always been there, even through the times when she had seemed able to forget it. And she knew now that it wasn't going to leave her, it had become her pet chameleon which when she left the prison would transform itself into a different shape. At least, though, she would be sharing it with Henry...

'A visitor for you, Mrs Trent.'

'Olga! Dear heart!'

'Oh, Pam!'

Sleep after all had crept back to her, encouraged perhaps by an ingredient of the coffee which had followed the cottage pie. But she wasn't in bed, just lying on it in her dressing-gown, and she slid off and met Pam as she crossed the room.

'Olga,' said Pam accusingly as they embraced, 'there's nothing of you!'

'Yes, I have lost a bit of weight, I realized just now... Oh, Pam.' *Goodbye, Pam, my best friend.* She remembered Pam teaching her that English idiom. When she had told Olga, suddenly solemn one day, that that was what she was. 'I'm so glad you've come.'

'I'm so glad you felt well enough to want

me... Oh Olga, what a mess, darling!'

'I know.' Suddenly, absurdly, she was in a panic. If Pam asked her any questions about Hugo, about what she had done and why, what she remembered... She hadn't rehearsed the answers with Henry.

'Don't worry, dear heart.' Pam was studying her face, seeing the anxiety in it. But that, of course, was what she would expect. 'I'm not going to ask you to talk about it. One day, when it's all over...' Pam smiled before looking round the room. 'It isn't bad in here, is it?'

'It's better than the remand cells,' said Olga, feeling almost cheerful in her relief. But she must try to control these sudden strong unfamiliar swings of mood. 'So is the food.'

'You're eating all right?'

'I suppose so. I'm not particularly interested in eating.'

'I suppose not...' Pam was studying her again.

'Pam, how are the children? Henry keeps telling me they're fine, but I can't help wondering...'

'They *are* fine, dear heart. I promise you. Henry hasn't brought them to see you?'

'No.' She had managed not to hesitate. 'He thought it was better...'

'Yes, of course.'

'Thanks for seeing so much of them.

283

Henry's told me how often you collect them from school, have them for tea.'

'Could you imagine me not doing?' asked Pam indignantly. The harsh lighting made her eyes very large and bright.

'Of course I couldn't. Oh, Pam, I'm so worried about them! I mean, the parents of other children at school, they'll talk to them, or at least in front of them, or the children will read the papers themselves and you know how cruel children can be...' In an hour – less than an hour – that worry would be done with too.

'They'll stand up for themselves,' said Pam. 'They don't think their mother has done anything terrible.' Pam's own curiosity came and went in her eyes. 'Children are so resilient.' She glanced down at her watch.

'What time is it?' asked Olga.

Pam's head jerked up, and there were a few unnerving seconds in which Olga didn't seem to recognize her. But she could hardly expect to recover completely, from her own terrors and the doctor's ministrations, in the space of a day. 'It's a quarter past three,' said Pam. She moved across to the one hard chair and sat down. 'Get back on the bed, dear heart,' she urged, 'and we'll just relax together for a moment. I'm afraid I can't stay long, I've got an appointment. But I felt I just had to see you.'

'That's how I felt,' said Olga. *Goodbye Pam,*

my best friend... 'Pam... Forgive me if I don't talk about it. I've always told you things–' except the thing she had told nobody – 'but with this... Perhaps one day...'

'Perhaps one day,' agreed Pam softly. Her small plump hands were probing at each other on her lap, the fingers lacing backwards and forwards. Olga didn't remember Pam's hands behaving like that. But there were probably several things she wouldn't remember. And wouldn't have the chance of rediscovering... A sudden vague sense of loss and cold honed down to one sharp image, and for a moment she couldn't speak.

'What is it, dear heart?' Pam was leaning towards her.

'Nothing. I was just wondering how Tommy was.' How Tommy would be when nobody came home. 'I'd forgotten all about him, poor old boy.'

'I went round at lunch-time yesterday, and he seemed fine,' said Pam indifferently. It had never been put into words between them, but Olga knew Pam didn't like animals. 'And the other weekdays when I went to see–'

'Oh, Pam! I might have known! You've peeled potatoes, given Tommy milk, I can just imagine it. Henry should have told me.'

'Men of our generation take such things for granted.' Pam laughed. 'It's all right, dear heart, I was only keeping an eye out, you would have done the same.'

'Yes… Oh, Pam, you are good.'

'It was nothing.' Pam glanced at her watch again. 'They seem to be managing all right. Henry said he was collecting the children from school today.'

'Yes…' In an hour's time the family would be together, out of reach.

Pam had got up and was walking about the room. 'What are you taking?' she asked, pausing by Olga's bedside table.

'Oh, it's only a tonic, some sort of Vitamin B mixture. Supposed to be good for the nerves.' They laughed together.

'What's this?' Pam picked up the black plastic oblong.

'That's my bell. It seems to work like a television remote control.'

'Ingenious,' said Pam, wandering back round the bed with the device in her hand. 'But not so good if the battery gave out when one was having a heart attack.' She sat down again.

'Don't press it by mistake,' said Olga, watching the restless hands.

'I won't, dear heart, don't worry.' Pam glanced at her watch again, then leaned towards the bed. 'Olga, I have to go now.'

'Oh, Pam. And I haven't told you how I appreciate…' This was something she should have said as soon as Pam arrived. 'What it means to me that you haven't changed, that you know why I'm here and yet you're still the same friend–'

'No, I haven't changed, Olga.'

'I can hardly bear to let you go.'

'You don't have to, dear heart,' said Pam. 'You're coming with me.'

'But, Pam…' Through the sudden whirl of her brain she grasped for the one continuous thread. So Pam was a colleague of Henry's and this was how he had arranged it. But why hadn't he prepared her?

'When Henry goes for the children this afternoon,' said Pam quickly and quietly, glancing yet again at her watch, 'in about fifteen minutes' time, he'll find out that they've already been collected. They're quite safe, Olga. So long as you do exactly as you're told.'

Pam bent down and put Olga's electronic bell on the floor. Then got up and stamped on it with one of her robustly shod small feet. Olga heard the crunch, and thought of the children's delicate bones. She had believed her supreme effort to hold herself together had already been made, but she was making it now.

'Just so that no one interferes with our plans. We're going home, Olga.'

'Home…'

'Back to Russia. Ten years has been a long time. For us both.'

'Brian…' She didn't know she had picked

Brian out from what had now become the snowstorm in her head, until she heard herself say his name.

'Brian?' repeated Pam contemptuously. 'No, not Brian. Just you and me.' She was rummaging in her capacious squashy handbag, bringing something out wrapped in patterned yellow paper like a bloated soap lemon. Taking the ribbon and the paper off. Holding up what looked like a khaki-coloured pineapple until Olga saw that it was a hand grenade.

Pam was showing it to her. 'Think about the children, Olga, and then follow my suggestions. Right?'

'Pam... Yes...' How could Pam still be looking as she had always looked, round rosy face radiant, eyes sparkling?

Because the Pam Olga thought she knew had never existed, the actress she was watching had merely reached the concluding stages of the performance she had put on ten years ago. Her hands, though, had signalled the denouement she had been preparing all that time...

'Good. Now I want you to behave as if you've chosen to come with me, Olga. As if I'm simply springing you from prison. I want them to think that they've got two women determined to get away. I think you'd better try and pull yourself together,' said Pam almost crossly, as she noticed that

Olga, although she had got off the bed and was standing up, was trembling from head to foot. 'I know you can. I had to admire the way you took that first telephone call, and then your actual instructions. But things have moved on since then – you'll be explaining things to us, Olga – and perhaps you need a boost.' Pam looked at her watch again. 'I didn't want to waste the time,' she murmured, 'but it looks as if... Sit down on the edge of the bed, Olga.'

She was sitting down, and Pam had rolled up one of her sleeves with her free hand. 'Remember the children,' said Pam, putting the grenade down on the chair and delving again into her handbag. 'This will actually make you feel a lot better.' Pam came back to the bed with a hypodermic syringe in her hand. Olga felt the needle, but not painfully. By the time Pam had returned the syringe to her bag and picked up the grenade again, the trembling had stopped and she had the strange sensation that she was watching herself as well as Pam.

'Right,' said Pam briskly. 'Up you get!'

They were face to face, or rather, Pam's head was just at Olga's chin level, if they were a few inches closer Olga would feel the soft fair hair... 'Pam,' Olga heard herself saying, 'Lucy *loves* you.'

'And you love Lucy,' said Pam, lifting her head to look at Olga. If only there could be something in Pam's eyes... But they were like pebbles.

'I thought you loved *me*,' said Olga, knowing the absurdity of it but that she must make one last attempt.

'There'll be time enough for love,' said Pam severely, 'when the world has been won by the people.'

So Pam was mad. Brilliantly, patiently, ideologically mad, but mad all the same. Somewhere behind Olga's terror the pain was very slightly less.

'We must go now,' said Pam.

'What use will I be to you?'

'They prefer people who disobey orders to be safely at home. Arrangements have been made to get me back, so it's very easy... And you just might be good for a swap. Take this.'

While she spoke Pam had been tearing at another prettily wrapped package, and she thrust a small revolver into the palm of Olga's right hand.

'But, Pam...'

'It's a replica,' said Pam impatiently. 'Think of the children and threaten to use it. Just follow me, I've learned everything about the way out from the hospital block since Henry told me you'd been brought here. When we get through the outer doors I'll lob the grenade back into the entrance and we'll run for the car.'

Despite the detachment Pam's needle had brought her, Olga had to swallow down a physical sickness. 'Pam, you can't…'

'I can and I will,' said Pam. 'Look, Olga.' The words and the few steps back from the door were a concession. 'We'll have plenty of time to talk later. All the time in the world. But at the moment we've got to act. If we don't, if we're not getting into the car at the moment agreed, with no one following us, Martin and Lucy will suffer. I'm sorry, but that's the arrangement, and there's no way now that it can be altered. Are you ready?'

'Yes,' said Olga, pointing the gun at Pam in illustration.

'Good!' Pam gave a brief professional smile which made Olga watch herself shudder. 'You only have to follow where I lead.'

'Goodbye,' Olga heard Pam say sweetly, before she herself was through the cell door. She came up behind Pam in time to see her free hand chop down on the neck of the man in uniform who had swivelled round to smile up at her. His eyes had glazed and he had fallen forward on to the desk before Olga was past him. What seemed to be keeping her moving was the thought of how Lucy's body looked as she hopped into the bath. Yet Pam had been right when she'd said the injection would make her feel better, she scarcely had a body of her own any more, she was floating after Pam, obedient on a reflex...

Pam was keeping up a steady pace, along corridors Olga was surprised to find deserted. There was no one else for Pam to disable until they reached the doors which led out to the main entrance lobby of the prison.

'Remember the children,' muttered Pam as they saw the two men in uniform standing in front of it. Relaxed men, chatting lazily to one another, but all at once one of them had tight hold of Pam while the other fielded the grenade from which she hadn't had time to draw the pin, and two more appeared from nowhere.

Pam was struggling and shouting and one of the two new men joined the first two to help restrain her, while the fourth, who wasn't in uniform, produced a hypodermic syringe, with which he managed after a few minutes to puncture her arm. Pam collapsed within seconds, and the man with the hypodermic turned to Olga just as a nurse came up behind her and took her by the waist.

'Are you all right?' asked the man and the nurse together.

'Yes. But my children... She said that if we didn't—'

'You're children are here,' said the man, 'waiting to see you. Shall I take that?'

Olga looked down at her hands and saw she was still holding the replica revolver. She offered it to him by the handle. 'It isn't real, she said I had to pretend–'

'I know.' The man put the gun into a pocket and took her wrist between his fingers, looking at her hard while he counted. 'All right,' he said to the nurse. 'Take her along now.'

'It's all over,' said the nurse encouragingly, as she and Olga turned and went slowly back to the hospital block. 'Don't look back.' When she did she couldn't see the woman who had been Pam, just a crowd of men round something which was on the floor by the doors.

'She hit the officer outside my room,' said Olga. 'I think she might have killed him.'

'She didn't actually,' said the nurse. 'But no skin off her nose.'

She brought Olga at last, after what felt a very long and tiring walk, into a room where she hadn't been before. It was quite large and properly furnished, and Henry, Martin and Lucy were there.

Henry went and sat down in a corner while she cuddled Lucy and then Martin. When she had an arm round them both he signalled to the nurse by the door, who invited the children to go with her to find some ice-cream. When she and Henry were alone – the nurse had closed the door

293

behind her and didn't come back – Olga realized she had to sit down, and Henry got up and came rather tentatively to stand in front of her, not touching her. After a silent moment he got down on his knees.

'No more horrors,' he said, 'I swear to you. Not even any more secrets, any more plans you won't know about. I expect you to be angry with me, even though there was no other way to bring it to an end. You see, Olga, the only way you could have known about Pam was if I'd told you. And if I *had* told you, it might just have shown and she mightn't have walked her way into our trap.'

'I think I must be very tough,' said Olga wearily.

'Strong,' corrected Henry, still not touching her.

'It was worse than anything else, but I can see you had to do it. How is it you knew about Pam and she didn't know about you?' She wasn't angry with him, she just felt reserved, and that he must be the one to put out a hand.

'We neither of us knew, I hadn't the wildest idea, but when I thought you'd been wakened up... In the jargon, Olga, you were a sleeper, someone waiting to be activated–'

'By the kiss of death,' said Olga, enjoying the exaggeration. 'Well, it almost was, Henry.'

'Oh, my darling.' She had thought, and

hoped, he would reach out to her. She met his hand half way.

'I didn't know I was a sleeper. But it wouldn't have made me feel any better if I had.' She was faintly cheered to hear herself make a poor little joke. 'Tell me how you found out about Pam.'

'As soon as I realized you'd been wakened I became pathologically suspicious of everyone I met. Excluding Pam at that point, not surprisingly. It was when we got back the night we'd been out for dinner, and Pam as so often was children-sitting. You remember?'

'Yes.' The timetable of those days was precise in her mind.

'You'd drunk a bit more than usual. I don't think I had, but I was pleased to encourage your comparatively cheerful mood for as long as I could. We got out of the car all mixed up together and laughing. I saw Pam's face. She could have been expected to look a bit disapproving, thinking of me driving, but she was looking – suspicious, watchful, calculating... Oh, a mixture of things which shouldn't have had anything whatsoever to do with that innocent moment. I suppose it takes one to know one. Not that I can say I suddenly knew about Pam. But I was suddenly going to find out. I had her under surveillance next morning.'

'Ian Bartholomew again?'

'No, I was able to get that investigation off the ground myself. But it was what we discovered about Pam that persuaded Ian to intervene with the police and get a murder investigation under way – we couldn't set her up until you were officially in the clear and could be quickly moved after her arrest to a place of absolute safety.'

'Obviously she hadn't the slightest suspicion about *you*. Don't you think they would have investigated you early on, when you wanted to marry me?'

'Of course they would. But I – we – were prepared for them. And ever since.'

'Oh, Henry...' And she had thought fear was her exclusive prerogative.

'Are you feeling better, darling?'

'I'm all right.'

'Good, we've got to go.'

'Now?' She had jumped to her feet and his arms were round her.

'Now. We've taken the people who were waiting for Pam – and you – at the gates. Their bosses will be waiting for *them*, to learn that Pam's mission was accomplished, so the sooner we're on our way the better.'

'Henry... She told me they were going to collect the children before you got there.'

'I've no doubt they were.' Her head was on his shoulder and he bent to kiss her hair. 'The children haven't been to school today. I went through the motions, drove in at the

In gate rather early, and stopped long enough round the bend for them to get down on the floor of the car under the rug. Then I drove on and through the Out gate. Martin and Lucy thought it was great fun.'

'Oh, darling...' There was a knock on the door, followed immediately by the appearance of a man Olga hadn't seen before.

'We're ready, sir,' said the man. He was carrying a coat, which he helped Olga into. It fitted her quiet well. The children followed him in and Lucy went dancing round the room.

'We're going in a helly copter!' she announced.

'There could just be someone else at the gates,' said Henry.

Prison buildings surrounded the small lawn where the helicopter was waiting. The pilot was already at the controls, and the man who had brought Olga the coat got in with them. The square of sky into which they climbed at right angles was pale blue, and as they cleared the buildings the setting sun streamed into Olga's eyes. It was hard to believe this was the end of the same afternoon in which she had last seen Pam.

'Do we take a plane now?' she asked Henry, as after no more than fifteen or twenty minutes the helicopter paused and began to descend.

'No,' said Henry. 'For the time being

we've arrived.'

'But you said exile…'

'So it is. You may not be far from home, but you won't be able to go shopping.'

'I wish I'd paid attention.' Believing their destination to be no more than a staging-post, she had watched the children rather than the earth below.

The lawn where they disembarked was larger than the one they had left, and beyond its three old stone walls there were fields. On the fourth side was the long high façade of a stately home. Three men were standing on the terrace, watching them.

'But Henry…' Olga envied the uncomplicated delight of Martin and Lucy.

'Let's go in,' said Henry.

Each with a child by the hand, and led by their fellow traveller, they climbed the stone steps between the stone urns from which the mauve and yellow faces of pansies were still turned towards them.

'Good to see you, Henry!'

One of the men advanced slightly towards them, and took Henry's hand. In the narrow gap created by his movement Olga saw a black cat sauntering out of the house. It wasn't Tommy but it made her think of him, clouding this moment of coming in from the cold. The children, with cries of pleasure, skirted the group of men and fell reverently to the ground in front of the cat, which permitted their tentative caresses.

'This is Jim Hargreaves,' Henry said to Olga.

'Welcome, Mrs Trent.' Jim Hargreaves transferred his hand. 'We'll take you straight to your room and you can rest. Then perhaps you'll feel like joining us for dinner. We hope you will.'

'Thank you. Lucy...'

'The children are all right, we'll bring them up eventually. Their rooms connect with yours.'

'Thank you.'

The staircase was wide and shallow, the large room looked over the lawn from which the helicopter had already vanished. Olga sat down on the window-seat as Henry opened the suitcases he must somehow have got out of the house.

'Henry, I've just thought of something. Not complaining, just curious. Why didn't you – they – arrest Pam as soon as she arrived at the prison? I mean, you must have known she would be carrying *something* incriminating. Didn't they search her?'

'Yes. They had to, of course, we couldn't risk her getting the least bit suspicious. But it was pretty sketchy, and she'd packaged her weaponry to outwit us. That on its own would have constituted an offence, of course, but not the almighty scandal which I'm confident will break in the media tomorrow.'

Henry grinned as he turned towards her. 'Needless to say your hospital room was bugged, and Pam, as we hoped, obligingly declared herself and her allegiance, and what she was going to do with her grenade. Our people were poised to rush in if it seemed you were in any immediate danger, but obviously it was of prime importance to Pam that you should leave your room on your own two feet and we weren't afraid of the injection we heard her giving you – although I'm glad I was advised not to listen in myself! I'm sorry about the man outside your room, but he was prepared to take the risk. The prison personnel, by the way, were replaced by our people, and it was all made as easy as possible for Pam consistent with not raising her suspicions. That's why the corridors were so empty.' Henry, who had done no more with the contents of the suitcases than strew them over the beds, sat down beside her, and seeing the shine of satisfaction in his eyes Olga realized how rare it was for him to reveal in his face so much of his state of mind. 'Now,' said Henry, 'with Pam disgraced and in custody, we can air your ten waiting years, and her role as your monitor. When we eventually get to bed we might amuse ourselves with a prophecy or two as to what tomorrow's headlines will actually be. I'm almost confident now, darling, that with everything coming out into the light our exile will begin and end in this house. We may want to move to escape the publicity, but it will be our choice. Pam, by the way, could be good for a swap.'

'You're wonderful, Henry. How I love you.' But there was still a little more than disuse to hold her back from utter happiness. 'Tommy, though. I'm sure Pam didn't particularly want to feed and water him, but at least she did.'

'I should have told you before, darling, I'm sorry – Mrs Metcalfe has Tommy. She loves him and it seemed the best thing. For the time being–'

'But Henry, the risk for her... They'll see it as the one possible link, maybe tap her telephone...'

'Not now. Remember we're on our way into the open. And anyway she's prepared for it. She does work for us from time to time.'

'Mrs Metcalfe! Fat, chatty, wheezy Mrs Metcalfe! Are you telling me she's been my minder?' Olga leaned towards Henry, seizing his face in her hands and starting to laugh in a way she could feel might turn into hysteria. 'All these years? No wonder you encouraged me to have a daily, told me the wife of that man on the train...'

'It wasn't all that much of a help,' said Henry, putting his hands up to encircle her wrists. 'Just someone to compare notes with now and then.'

'You never saw her!' She had to try harder and harder to contain her laughter.

'We talked on the telephone. She rang to report the change in you.'

'Mrs Metcalfe!'

Through the crescendo of the noise she was making there came a knock on the door. It might have sobered her, but Henry took his hand off her arm and slapped her sharply on the cheek. Then in the abrupt silence leaned forward to kiss the stinging spot.

'Come!' he called, helping her to her feet and leading her by the hand across the room.

The door opened and a man walked in. A familiar man, only this was the first time she had seen life in the eyes which instantly found hers, felt the warm strength of the hand.

As she gazed back, aware that joy and relief were chasing the shock out of her face, the man began to smile and his other hand came up to reinforce the pressure round hers.

'Someone else safely arrived to enjoy the hospitality of the house,' said Henry cheerfully. 'I don't really have to introduce you two, do I, but I'll go through the motions. My wife Olga – Ian Bartholomew!'

The publishers hope that this book has given you enjoyable reading. Large Print Books are especially designed to be as easy to see and hold as possible. If you wish a complete list of our books please ask at your local library or write directly to:

Dales Large Print Books
Magna House, Long Preston,
Skipton, North Yorkshire.
BD23 4ND

This Large Print Book, for people
who cannot read normal print,
is published under the auspices of

THE ULVERSCROFT FOUNDATION